GU01017945

A HOWL
OF
ANGUISH

Janice Hutchings

Published by

**MELROSE
BOOKS**

An Imprint of Melrose Press Limited
St Thomas Place, Ely
Cambridgeshire
CB7 4GG, UK
www.melrosebooks.co.uk

FIRST EDITION

Copyright © Janice Hutchings 2016

The Author asserts her moral right to
be identified as the author of this work

Cover by Melrose Books

ISBN 978-1-911280-63-7
epub 978-1-911280-64-4
mobi 978-1-911280-65-1

All rights reserved. No part of this publication may be reproduced, stored in a retrieval
system, or transmitted, in any form or by any means electronic, mechanical, photocopy-
ing, recording or otherwise, without the prior permission of the publishers.

This book is sold subject to the condition that it shall not, by way of trade or otherwise,
be lent, re-sold, hired out or otherwise circulated without the publisher's prior consent
in any form of binding or cover other than that in which it is published and without a
similar condition including this condition being imposed on the subsequent purchaser.

Printed and bound in Great Britain by:

Lightning Source UK Ltd, Chapter House, Pitfield

Kiln Farm, Milton Keynes, MK11 3LW

Chapter 1

As she stirred in her sleep, the sound of church bells penetrated her senses, a momentary flicker of the eyelids and Marjorie was awake. *What day is it?* she asked herself. Of course, it's Sunday. I can do what I like. With no need to get up, she lay for while, thinking of nothing in particular. After a while, the bells fell silent, only to be replaced by the church clock striking the hour.

She sat up, yawning and stretching, she climbed out of bed. The room stuffy, she stepped to the window to let in the soft morning air.

A wasp caught in the folds of the curtain put up a desperate fight for life.

Unperturbed, Marjorie having trapped it sent it on its way through the open window.

For a while she stood by the sill, to take in the scenery.

A pall of mist hanging over gardens and neighbouring roofs cloaked the little market town of Stonebridge. She could just make out the ghostly outline of the ancient oak at the bottom of the garden. Although not visible, the mingled scents of honeysuckle and summer roses sprinkled with morning dew, assailed her nostrils.

From the kitchen below, a clatter of cutlery and a savoury smell of bacon and eggs sizzling in the frying pan, with a few field mushrooms picked the previous day, stimulated her gastric juices.

She stood in front of the wash basin, studying her reflection in the mirror above it she brushed her fair hair vigorously, drawing it back with a velvet ribbon. She washed her face and brushed her teeth. What would she wear today? Her favourite T-shirt, the one her brother Tim, who was in the Army, had given her. A surprise gift from Thailand.

The T-shirt, a multi-coloured affair depicting temple dancers against a black background, with a pair of worn denim jeans and plimsolls, she considered the height of fashion.

With these thoughts in mind, and a last look in the mirror, she made her way down to the kitchen.

'Morning Ma, that smells good.' Marjorie sat at the table, picking up her knife and fork, she eyed the eggs and bacon on the plate in front of her. 'Where's the mushrooms? … I'm starving.'

'I don't know where 'e puts it. I gave 'em to your father, 'e fancied 'em.' Mary, Marjorie's mother, pursed her lips. 'You know what it is, anything to keep the peace.'

Her father, for once in a good mood, smiled good-humouredly. Charles Henderson enjoyed being the centre of attention. Since the accident, on a daily basis, with an eagle eye, he could be found in his wheelchair by the range monitoring the comings and goings.

'Once the mist clears, it should be another fine day.' Mary, standing at the range, glanced over her shoulder at her daughter. 'Get that down 'e while it's hot so I can clear away the dishes. Gran's coming today, and 'er likes everything neat and tidy.'

'I wouldn't say no to more.' Charles, eyeing Marjorie's plate, licked his lips.

'Oh go on with 'e,' Mary started to clear the table. 'Find something to do, read a book or something.'

'I ain't got a book.'

'Then 'e'll have to wait until Mother comes with the Sunday paper.'

Turning to Marjorie, Mary said, 'I see you've finished, dear, how 'bout a nice cup of tea to round it off?'

'Not now, thank you Ma, I'll have one later on.' Marjorie, placing her fork and knife together on the plate, handed it to her mother.

'I wouldn't say no to a cup of tea.' Charles wasn't going to be left out.

'Can I help with the dishes?' Marjorie, getting up, pushed back the kitchen chair.

'No, leave 'em to me, dear.' At the sink, Mary, piling the

dirty crockery into a plastic bowl, reached for the washing up liquid. 'But 'e could take some rubbish down to the bin an' check on the hens.'

'What 'bout me cup of tea, Mary ol' girl, 'tis a long time coming.'

Her mother had a lot to put up with, Marjorie thought, as closing the back door, her father's voice still ringing in her ears, petulant and demanding.

*

Marjorie, picking her way along the stony path to the henhouse, found the garden very much overgrown. The fact it was high summer offered no excuse for its tangled state. The heat of the sun, having burnt off the mist, stood out like a sore thumb. Myriad insects swarming in the humid atmosphere buzzed in the long grasses lining the way. Shrubs and bushes, once her mother's pride and joy, were now engulfed in weeds and strangled by ivy. The garden had lost its identity and was fast becoming a wilderness.

In the past, its upkeep had presented no problem, and had even given moments of pleasure, but not now, with Tim in the Army and Dad a permanent invalid – after the forklift truck at work had dropped its load, near to where he was working. Of course, he'd been compensated for the accident, but the money he received could hardly be compared with his regular earnings.

An active man, he had become embittered and given to sudden rages and mood swings. The doctor would have prescribed tranquillizers to alleviate the problem, but he would have none of it.

'I won't be doped,' he'd say.

Marjorie, on nearing the end of the path leant back against the gnarled trunk of the oak tree. A relic of her childhood and friend of longstanding, its canopy of leaves fluttered in a welcome breeze, in its shade the hen house and chicken run. She had emptied the rubbish, and was rummaging for eggs, in the fusty coop, amid clucking and broody hens, when she'd heard a noise. A cat emerged from the overgrown bushes at the side of the path, its tail erect, purring on its approach it wrapped itself around her legs.

'Hello Puss, where did you spring from?'

At the sound of her voice, the cat extended its spiral welcome, then, tiring, lay down in the long grasses.

Marjorie made her way back, fully expecting the cat to follow her. But it stayed where it was.

Her mother looked up as, lifting the latch, she stepped into the kitchen.

'Back love …' she smiled. 'I see 'e's collected some eggs.'

'Yes, there were more than I thought there would be,' said Marjorie, placing the basket on the table.

Mary glanced at the wall clock, 'It's time 'e got ready for church, Gran will be 'ere soon.'

'I hope 'er won't forget the Sunday paper.' Charles, flustered and red-faced, scanned the floor. 'Where's me slippers? I can't find 'em anywhere.'

Chapter 2

Amelia Tucker mused as seeing her reflection in the hall stand mirror. It wasn't that she didn't understand her son-in-law's dilemma, but in her opinion, his persistent wallowing in self-pity served no purpose and was completely self-destructive.

The air in the hall was oppressive. She felt overdressed in her Sunday clothes, but respectable for Church. It would be expected of her. To her, her best tweed suit and hat, and feather to match, with highly polished leather shoes should serve the purpose.

From the hall stand, she picked up her leather handbag and drawing on her kid gloves, opened the front door and stepped outside.

The mist clearing had made way for the sun. Not a leaf stirred on the trees lining the pavements. On the corner could be seen the stray dog, as usual daring anyone to come near it.

She locked the front door and set off down the road. She had only gone a few yards when she realised she had forgotten to bring the Sunday paper. 'No, not again, what a nuisance. I'll have to go back an' get it,' she muttered, retracing her steps.

Minutes later, Amelia, on rounding the corner, saw her daughter's cottage. An habitual feeling of despair and hopelessness engulfed her when seeing the peeling paint and the overgrown front garden. Even so, Mary always looked on the bright side – she always managed to smile and welcomed her with a hug, she could count on that.

Mary and Marjorie were standing at the gate waiting for her,and with the Sunday paper dutifully delivered, the three of them set off for church.

*

The ten o'clock communion service was always well attended by the inhabitants of the little market town, with farmers coming in from the outlying areas, it lasted just over an hour.

The church, a small one, aptly named "The Good Shepherd" welcomed its flock on Sundays. It provided a place after the service in the church hall with tea, coffee and biscuits, a meeting place to share in the latest gossip, catch up on the news, or simply renew old acquaintances.

The church, on the edge of the town, lay hidden away behind a farm and was well surrounded by trees.

A Norman Church with a *trefoil piscine* and the royal coat of arms of George III, it was approached by a long, insignificant lane bordering the farm drive. In this church, Marjorie had been christened in the plain Norman font shaped like a large egg-cup with a lead interior.

However, because of the church's proximity, a longer walk retracing the lane after the service was necessitated in order to reach the church hall and the public house, "The Lion's Lair", a popular venue, a little way down the road.

As always, on their approach, with the church coming into sight, Marjorie thought of her Dad's allotment, one of many at the back, giving way to open fields.

On a Saturday when out for a walk or homeward bound from Ruby's, her school friend's house, she would pay a visit, only to find the once well tended rows of vegetables over-run by a confusion of long grasses, brambles and weeds. Now it was a veritable paradise for the local cat population – if on a hunting expedition for field mice. Disheartened, she would turn away, as if closing her eyes would make the problem go away.

At one time, when arranging flowers in the church, in the silence and alone, she had knelt and prayed for the help so sorely needed to overcome her father's disability.

'How are you, my dear, and how are the family coping?' After the service, although in a meditative mood, she would have recognised that voice anywhere, knowing it belonged to The Rev. Jeremiah Makepiece. He was standing in his customary place in the church porch, his kind and benevolent face, showing the concern and sympathy she had so grown accustomed to.

She glanced in the direction of her mother and Gran, some way away, in earnest conversation with a Mrs Blacker, a long-term and valued friend of Gran's.

'I feel so sorry for Ma,' she said. 'She works so hard and worries so much. At times I feel helpless, but I must and will help her.' Marjorie didn't mention the lack of money, but their plight was obvious to all.

Jeremiah, drawing her aside, confided, 'If I or anyone else can help in any way, you know you only have to ask.'

'Thank you,' Marjorie, managing a smile, knew her mother would never accept any kind of help.

*

The Sunday paper slipped to the floor as Charles Henderson relaxed his grip. The bottled beer his mother-in-law had brought him nearly gone, he felt tired and somewhat bored. The sports column of no further interest, he closed his eyes, the silence bearing down upon him, he felt very much alone.

He listened to the various sounds coming in from the garden, as only these penetrated and broke the stillness. Soft breezes ruffling the kitchen curtains, the open window swinging gently to and fro on its catch, the buzzing of various insects and in the distance the clucking of hens – his hens, a welcomed diversion.

Somewhere a cat lodged a noisy objection with an adversary. Tibby maybe defending her territory.

After a while, he heard the cat scratching on the back door. The stray tabby they had adopted – or had it adopted them?

Opening his eyes just for a moment, forgetting his limitations or merely choosing to dismiss his infirmity, he foolishly tried to get out of his enforced prison to let Tibby in. This having failed, he then attempted to manoeuvre the wheelchair to the door. This too having failed, to his dismay, only succeeding in knocking over the beer bottle and spilling its last precious drops on the carpet. Not that he cared about the carpet, but the beer, what a waste!

He turned on the little radio, thoughtfully placed within easy reach by Marjorie. He leant back and closed his eyes in an attempt to savour the music and let it flow over him in an effort to escape the depression, which always encompassed him when aware of his own vulnerability.

He mused and dreamed of his life as a supervisor in the market garden warehouse where he had worked for so many years. Voices long forgotten now brought to mind, so familiar. The atmosphere … the forklift truck, the urgency, the fear, impending danger, panic, the violence, the shouting and then … 'Charles, wake up! It's Mary.'

The voice seemed a long way away, panic-stricken and perspiring Charles reaching out, attempted to struggle and fight his way away from the imagined threat.

The voice, louder now, joined by others, persisted, 'Charles, wake up! It ain't nothing but a dream.' With the veil dropping, his befuddled brain became aware of an image, a face, Mary's face. She was kneeling in-front of him, holding his hand; standing behind her and looking concerned were his mother-in-law and Marjorie.

Chapter 3

The following Thursday, travelling home on the school bus, Marjorie gazed unseeingly out at the passing countryside, the wayside houses and the occasional outbuilding. She was so absorbed in her thoughts, such images left no impact or meaning.

'Is it something I've said?' Ruby, her friend, sitting alongside her, prodded her in the ribs. 'I hate talking to myself …' A thought occurred; 'If it's the exams you're worried about, you've no need to be.'

'Thank you.'

Ruby's remark had merited only a perfunctory response.

At that moment, a paper missile from the back of the coach landed on Marjorie's lap.

'Take no notice of him, he's a menace,' Ruby said emphatically. 'He'll be the ruination of my brother.'

Fourteen-year-old Harry Jenkins, to whom Ruby referred, lived for the moment and had no scruples as to whom he hurt in the process. With his older brother, Oliver, now away at College, his unruly nature had taken a turn for the worse, not only that – to Ruby's dismay – her younger brother, James, looked up to him.

The atmosphere in the coach was hot and uncomfortable, Marjorie, very much aware of the noisiness of her fellow schoolmates – some of whom she thought were chatting inanely about trifles – wiped the condensation from the window pane in an attempt to peer out. A thin, misty rain was dampening the roads and hedgerows, steam rising from the surrounding countryside. The sky darkened to a gunmetal grey, indicating a change in the weather, the like of which prompted Archie Reynolds, the bus driver, to switch on his headlights and window wipers. The latter made an irritating screeching noise.

As they travelled along, the misty rain intensified, the bus sending up spray from numerous puddles in the lanes. On approaching the outskirts, the nameplate for Stonebridge was barely discernible.

'This one's got a message on it.' Another missile landed at Ruby's feet. She picked it up. 'What a cheek, listen to this, he says, "You know you like me, not many girls can resist my charm and good looks." Good looks and charm, indeed,' snorted Ruby. 'Who does he think he is?'

Marjorie looked back over her shoulder. Harry, sat in the back seat, a smug expression on his face, caught her eye. He winked disdainfully; she turned away.

As the bus slowed down on arrival, the inevitable scramble for the exit was on the cards, much to Archie's consternation.

'See you tomorrow, Marj.' Ruby, living on the outskirts, got out along with the others.

The school bus stopped twice; once on the outskirts and once in the centre of the market town. To Marjorie's relief, Harry Jenkins got out at Ruby's stop.

She glanced out the window and waved to Ruby, who – as most of them – was taken unawares by a change in the weather, without a mackintosh or umbrella, was bracing herself for the race back home.

The group quickly disbanded and Ruby, rounding a corner, in the swirling mist, soon vanished from sight.

Moments later, wet and bedraggled, Marjorie made her way up the garden path. A light blazed from the front room window, sending out a homely glow over the dampened footpath and shrubberies.

Huddled in the porch was a dark shape. On her approach, Tibby, her wet fur matted and covered in mud, mewed a welcome, at the same time proudly presenting her with a field mouse, her offering for the day.

'Where have you been? I don't want that!' Marjorie, disgusted, averted her eyes.

Marjorie opened the door. Tibby, in disgrace, followed her in. The warm kitchen appeared to greet her like an old friend, with its cosy interior and cooking smells – she was glad to be home.

Thursday night was Mary's whist night. Her mother, this time in a mackintosh, was dressed ready to meet Grandma at the bus stop. They would catch the bus to the outskirts where the whist drive was held in the church hall.

'My, you are soaking, dear, take off those wet clothes and wipe yourself dry. You'll find some clean towels in the airing cupboard.' Mary, drawing on her gloves, picked up her umbrella. She gasped as Tibby sidled up to her, 'And that cat, where's it been and what's it got in its mouth? A mouse! Get rid of it.'

'I thought I had.' Marjorie, not relishing the task in hand, mustered up a smile.

'Afore I forget, there's some stew from yesterday's leftovers simmerin' on the range. Dad's in the front room reading the paper; 'e shouldn't be much trouble, just take him in 'e's mug of tea, strong with plenty of sugar, during the evenin', with a few biscuits. Now, was there anything else?' She cast her eyes around the room. 'Oh yes, don't forget to shut them hens up for the night. I've put out some milk and scraps for Tibby. Now where did I put me purse with the loose change in it?' Mary, panic stricken, rummaged. 'Would you believe it, it wos in me pocket all the time. I'd better go, mustn't keep Gran waitin'.'

On completing the various tasks allotted to her, Marjorie pondered. Should she keep Dad company and try and engage him in conversation. She would have thought it was in his interest. He should not cut himself off from others, as he was doing with her this evening, in the other room. But if in one of his moods, any attempt by Ma or herself to ease his pain, it seemed, was misinterpreted and treated with suspicion; a suspicion that locked him in a solitary prison, a prison of which he only had the key.

She thought of the times before the accident and found it difficult to associate the withdrawn, sullen man, prone to sudden rages, with the happy-go-lucky father with a protective streak, who had loved life. The one who had joined in all the family activities with relish. She had so many happy memories of him on family outings, sharing each other's problems and always being there. Why, why did fate take a hand, to change him in

11

such a traumatic way? So many questions with no answers or explanations.

She shrugged her shoulders and, shaking her head, dismissed what she thought an unanswerable problem … yet was it unsolvable? Surely something could be done.

Later that evening, Marjorie, looking in on her father, found him asleep in his wheelchair. He looked so peaceful that she took care not to disturb him.

She gently smoothed his brow and, switching off the radio, was just about to leave the room when she noticed the evening paper lying on the floor. She picked it up and was about to fold it when a caption in the Situations Vacant column caught her eye. It read, "Wanted, Saturday Girl".

*

Marjorie, wandering around the garden centre, couldn't believe her good fortune.

Only a short moment ago she had been waiting, for what seemed an eternity, outside the administration manager's office. Nervous and apprehensive, when sitting outside a door with "Mr M. Blackler" on it, when the door opened she was surprised to see an office no larger than a cupboard.

She guessed Mr Blackler, once dark-haired but now greying and aged, to be about forty years old. He smiled and informed her that his name was Mike. As he interviewed her, she noticed that there were many vacancy notices, full and part-time, pasted on a board attached to the wall behind him. Marjorie relaxed when he reassured her that her lack of experience was of no concern to him as she would be under supervision for a short space of time until she learned the ropes. The manager, impressed with her appearance and personality, rose from his chair and announced that the job was hers if she wanted it, starting the next Saturday, with a view to long-term employment when leaving school, if she so wished. He had taken her name and address, and discussing the wages with her, had wished her well in her new job.

*

The Oasis Garden Centre & Nurseries on the outskirts of Stonebridge, for which Marjorie would be working in the gift department, was a large concern, catering for many needs. A recent addition to ever increasing developments, it was relatively new but nevertheless a welcome attraction on a day out.

Marjorie, sitting in the restaurant with a cup of coffee as it was too early to catch the bus home, was thinking how pleased Ma would be on hearing the news, the agreed sum of three pounds ten shillings an hour would help to ease their financial plight.

'May I share your table?'

Marjorie looked up. The speaker, a dark-haired young man with a pleasant expression, was standing in-front of her.

'Please do.' She indicated the chair opposite to her. 'My name's Marjorie. I've just been taken on. I'm to work in the gift shop on Saturdays.'

'A very welcome addition, I'm sure. By the way, my name's Malcolm, and strangely enough so am I, but full-time and have been for quite a while.'

Marjorie blushed. Malcolm was good-looking and although he was a stranger, as they conversed, she found herself enjoying his company.

So much so that time flew. Glancing at her watch, she said, 'I'm sorry, I'll have to go, I've a bus to catch.'

Malcolm, seemingly disappointed, managed a smile. 'What, already?' he said in a light-hearted way. 'Just as I'm getting to know you. If I hadn't been working, I could have run you home on my Lambretta.'

In the bus on the way home, an image of Malcolm's face lingered in her mind. Would he speak to her again, she wondered, or was it just one of those things that happened? Hopefully not.

Chapter 4

Harry Jenkins, sitting on the old stone wall with nothing to do, was bored. His brother away at University – *more fool him*, he thought. He'd had enough of learning in stuffy classrooms with bossy teachers.

James, alongside him, was fiddling with a pair of old binoculars, he had found at home in the attic.

To Harry, his so-called friend had become a pain in the neck, 'Give 'em to me,' he cried.

'No 'e'll break 'em.' James might have known his remark would fall on deaf ears – Harry never listened to him.

'I said, give 'em to me!' Harry snatched the binoculars and with a teasing look, held them aloft out of James' reach. He laughed, and waving them around, released his grip.

'Now look what 'e's done!' James, solemn-faced, scrambled down off the wall to retrieve them ''E's broke 'em!'

'They ain't any use, anyway. Wot's there to see round 'ere?'

'There's …' James put on his thinking cap. 'There's birds. I've seen a fox through 'em, but I won't anymore, will I?' He knelt to tie up a shoelace which was always coming undone. 'Anyway, us should 'ave gone to school, it being Friday, I thought it didn't matter, but it did. Ruby told me Ma, 'er didn't see me on the bus. I wos sent to me room.' Tight-lipped he sat on the grass, deep in thought. His sister had told him not to mix with Harry, and now he was beginning to wish he had listened to her.

'Cor, it ain' half hot, wot's us going to do now?' Harry, having wiped the perspiration from his face with a grubby handkerchief, shaded his eyes from the sun.

''Ow do I know? Throw some more stones at the dog, I suppose. But I'm not goin' to this time, it's cruel.'

'My, wot a lengthy speech.' Harry sneered. 'It ain't anything special, it's only a stray. Nobody wants it.'

James frowned. 'One day, it'll bite you …'e'll see.'

'So wot!' Harry shrugged his shoulders. 'I'm off, coming? Ouch …!' his hand brushed against a stinging nettle as he joined James in the dusty lane.

'Might as well, I suppose.' James bent down to pick up the binoculars. 'Where we goin' anyway?'

'My place, I've something to show 'e.' Harry, pained by the nettle, was sucking his finger.

'Wot?'

James was hooked, as Harry had known he would be.

'Wouldn't 'e like to know? … Come on, slow coach.' Harry wasted no time, now some way ahead, he looked back and beckoned.

James hesitated, then against his better judgement, trailed after him.

Unbeknown to them, at that moment, sitting on its haunches and observing them from a distance, the stray dog, seeing the boys disappear, raised its head to the sky and howled as if in anguish.

*

Harry, obsessed with his latest craze, purposely hurried on, now and then looking back to see if James was still following him. Ruby, in his opinion, was turning James into a first-class sissy. Fancy being bossed around by a girl! She was always telling him what he should or should not do. Given time, he thought, being seen in James' company might do some irreversible damage to his macho image.

The sky now overcast, he was glad it wasn't so hot. With the heat he had felt languid and irritable.

James catching up, panting and out of breath, gasped, ''E could have waited for me?'

'Wait fer 'e? By the time 'e makes up yer mind, what youm doing, it ain't worth doing.'

'I've been thinking …' James hesitated.

'You've been thinking wot?'

'I've been thinking I don't think I'll come. I think I'll go 'ome. Anyway it's startin' to drizzle.'

''Fraid of getting wet, you pansy? Going 'ome now … it ain't dark.' Harry shrugged his shoulders. 'I don't know what I'm goin' to do with you.'

James hung his head. Torn between Ruby and Harry, he couldn't make up his mind. But he didn't want to lose face. 'O.K., I'll come, but I don't want any trouble like last time.'

'Oh that, how wos I to know somebody was in the 'ouse when I climbed in the winda? Anyway, 'e'll like wot I'm goin' to show 'e now.'

The battered old garden gate creaked as Harry, pushing it open, led the way through the long grasses to a shed in the corner. He looked back then with a mischievous grin, and a wink, unlatched the door and disappeared inside.

James, wondering what was in there, approached with caution. He stood in the doorway and peered in. His eyes having adjusted to the dim interior, he gasped on seeing a powerful motorbike with red bodywork and the name "Honda" emblazoned in gold on one side; its highly polished chrome catching the light from a makeshift grimy window.

'What a smasher!' James couldn't believe his eyes. 'Whose is it?' A dark thought occurred. He frowned, 'It ain't stolen, is it!'

'Course not, it's me brother's, wot do 'e take me fer!' Harry, with an impatient gesture, climbed on the seat. 'Wot luck, the key's in the ignition.' He gripped the handlebars,'E's not around to see, if I 'ave a go, is 'e? Us will go fer a run, once I've found some leathers.'

'But 'e can't drive, Harry …'

'I won't tell anyone, if 'e don't. You'm no chicken, are 'e?' Harry, just like Kenneth Grahame's Toad of Toad Hall, bluffed his way out of a dangerous situation.

*

Freckled-faced and red-haired, Harry Jenkins was the image of Uncle Patrick. His uncle, without any ties, now in the Merchant Navy, had been known to hit the bottle and run foul of the law.

Robert, Harry's father, now having none of his brother's restlessness and need to travel, with a steady job, had married Pam, and settled down.

Oliver, their eldest son, dark-haired like his father and similar in looks, personified his mother's mentality, her desire to succeed in life at all costs. The odd one out, Harry, refusing to accept any advice or guidance, had turned his back on his family, and just like his uncle, had taken to wandering around making a nuisance of himself.

Oliver was away at university. The wayward Harry, without his brother's sobering influence, was in seventh heaven. He could do what he liked.

With a disdainful look and a cursory glance at James' receding figure, Harry, helmeted, wheeled the bike, heavy as it was, through the long, straggly grass to the garden path. On reaching the gate, he kicked it open, then, guiding the machine onto the kerbside, propped it up. There, he adjusted his visor and with a nonchalant gesture, turned on the ignition.

*

James, his ego at its lowest ebb with nothing better to do, picked up a stout stick to thrash the wet hedgerows in a vain attempt to relieve his tension.

On rounding a bend, a rabbit, startled by his activities, fled across his path. Wide-eyed, its powder-puff tail signalling danger, it plunged into thick undergrowth just in front of him.

His head bent against sheets of misty rain, he trudged along, stopping now and then to pull up his socks and tie up the infuriating shoelace.

His hair sticking to his scalp, he wiped moisture from his face with a rather grubby handkerchief. He stopped to get his bearings, only to find he still had some way to go. The mist and driving rain impeding his progress, his shoes slopping with water, he plodded on.

Home at last, the misty rain had ceased, the sky clearer, brighter, not so foreboding. A recognised "mew" in the form of a welcome greeted him with the next door's cat padding up the path to greet him.. An affectionate little thing, as black as coal, aptly named Blackie, it was purring for all its worth.

'Where have you been?' Ruby, in the kitchen, laying the table for tea, was not in a good mood. 'Up to no good, I'll be bound, with that Harry Jenkins!'

James, avoiding eye contact, remained silent.

She frowned. 'Well, take off those wet clothes and make yourself useful. Dad and Ma will be home soon.'

Chapter 5

Marjorie, although absorbed in her job in the gift shop, had tried to catch Malcolm's eye when seeing him occasionally in such close promimity. But he deliberately ignored her. His indifference puzzled her. It was like they'd never met or spoken to one another.

She was losing heart. He obviously wasn't interested in her. She had seen him talking to a number of girls, one in particular. She found herself taking her coffee break alone, or with newly made female friends, even though, on numerous occasions, she had taken care to seat herself at the table where first they'd met.

One afternoon, on an occasion such as this, immersed in a magazine, she became aware of a presence. On looking up, she was surprised to see Malcolm standing in-front of her as before. To see him at that moment, to her, seemed almost like a rerun of an old film.

Malcolm, totally unaware of her reaction, smiled and said in his old familiar way, 'May I share your table?'

At the sound of his voice, her heart raced, pulling herself together and trying to look composed, she said, 'Please do, my name's Marjorie, I've just been taken on. I'm to work in the gift shop on Saturdays.'

Malcolm, at first surprised and bewildered, suddenly burst out laughing, much to the consternation and interest of those seated at the surrounding tables, but even so, the ice had been broken between them.

That day, the sun receded behind the clouds, the hot, muggy day giving way to a misty drizzle.

'There's no need to spray all the plants at the moment,' commented Angie, who worked in the flower shop.

The two of them were standing together in a queue at the bus stop.

Marjorie, revelling in the soft misty rain, lifted her face skywards. She was in seventh heaven when thinking of Malcolm that afternoon in the Tea Shop, perhaps she would see him there again.

'Are you listening to me, Marjorie, there's some fellow trying to attract your attention. I should be so lucky.' Angie's voice broke this train of thought.

Am I dreaming, she thought. Malcolm, astride a metallic-gold Lambretta, was asking her if she would like a lift.

'I thought you'd never ask,' she said. Her heart pounding, her cheeks aglow, she took the helmet he handed her and climbed on behind him.

'Hold tight,' Malcolm said.

She held on to the seat. The machine roared into life. She felt the thrill of the experience for the first time as they took to the road.

'Alright?' He cried, with a rush of misty rain, and the noise of the engine.

'Yes, it's fun!' *More than fun*, she thought. *My dream's come true. But I wonder what Ma would think. Dad would never forgive me, that's for sure. Come to think of it, Malcolm doesn't know where I live.*

*

Malcolm knew, with thick drizzle and poor visibility, it was not the best of conditions to take to the road. Spits and spots of rain speckled a visor, already clouded by his breath, prompting him to flip it open, consequently exposing his face to drifts of fine rain.

The way ahead, obscured by the mist, shadowy outlines emerged when least expected. Residues of water from hedge-rows, seeping from fields within, pocketed the road with numerous puddles on road surfaces,already treacherous due to a long dry spell.

Clasping her hands around Malcolm's waist, Marjorie was well aware of his concern. His body tense, he focused on the road ahead. Shielded, she occasionally flipped up her visor with a view to getting a truer picture of the conditions, and it was whilst doing so she spotted a motorcyclist in the headlights of a passing car. On a grassy verge near a bend in the road some way ahead, the rider was sitting astride his machine.

Broken down, she thought, *and in such weather*. Out of sheer curiosity, she glanced at the motorcyclist. He or she appeared to be fiddling with the controls. In one fleeting moment, as they spun past, she caught a glimpse of a face, the face of Harry Jenkins. Surprised and concerned, a thought occurred – no good would come of this encounter, suppose he had spotted her.

After a while, Malcolm, pulling into the side of a verge, commented, 'I'm going back, that guy's got problems, maybe I can help him.'

'No!' Marjorie froze at the thought.

Taken aback by her reaction, Malcolm said, 'Really Marjorie, that's not very public-spirited.'

'Don't do it, don't, I beg of you!'

'Why, Marjorie, do you know him?'

'Yes.'

Marjorie upset, Malcolm pressed no further. She would, he thought, tell him in her own good time.

He started up the bike. Marjorie's mood had changed: at first, light-hearted, she had now become subdued.

The drizzle had eased and with the grey sky lightening up, the visibility and conditions improved. Malcolm, glancing in his wing mirror, saw only a solitary car behind him.

The next moment, on approaching a bend in the road, Malcolm spotted the motorcyclist behind him. He was some way off, driving erratically at speed. He said nothing, but kept a watchful eye.

Rounding the bend, he glanced again in the mirror, fully expecting to see the rider close behind him. But there was no sign. He became complacent, not bothering to look again for a while. But when he eventually did, he saw the rider close behind, apparently in pursuit.

In desperation, he increased his speed, at the same time, taking stock of his pursuer in the mirror.

'What's wrong?' Marjorie broke the tension. 'It's him isn't it. Don't take any risks.'

Malcolm, focusing on the progress of his pursuer, failed to see the dog until it was too late.

Chapter 6

Charles, sat in his wheelchair listening to his radio. He turned it off, then closed his eyes; its dulcet tones had done little to alleviate his troubled mind.

He roused himself, and having drained the last drops of beer in the bottle, put on his spectacles in order to complete an unfinished crossword. *Good for the little grey cells*, he thought, but try as he might, his second attempt proved as frustrating as the first. The unresolved puzzle leaving him with feelings of inadequacy, he tossed his glasses aside.

The radio off, the room seemed unbearably quiet, he could almost hear a pin drop. The only sounds being the steady tic of the hall clock, with an occasional snore from the basket in the corner.

He sighed. To him, it seemed such a long time since Mary, promising to be back soon, had gone out. He never would have thought he would come to this. Once a proud man, he was no longer in control.

At least, he thought, the weather was improving, for up to now it had not looked at all promising. A glimpse or two out of the window earlier had revealed a grey, overcast sky, which had done nothing to lift his spirits. With a misty rain and a damp-ening of the windowpanes, the branches of an apple tree were barely visible in the gloom.

At that moment, the table lamp, which had been attached to a timing device, came on, its warm glow lighting up the room. Tibby, momentarily disturbed, stretched, then, with a series of turns, settled down in her basket.

Charles, fumbling once again for his glasses, wheeled himself over and switched on the television.

The news, just as he'd known it would be, was quite depress-ing. Amongst other things, there had been a road accident –

a smack-up between a powerful motorcycle and a smaller bicycle or scooter. 'Shouldn't be on the road,' he muttered, turning off the set.

What shall I do now? He asked himself. *I know, I'll have another stab at that crossword.* He picked up the paper and studied the clues. A quarter of an hour elapsed; he'd almost finished it, but for a final clue. An unanswerable clue, apparently, for, beaten, he had given up in despair.

He switched on the television to take his mind off things, this time selecting a documentary entitled *Animals of the Wild*.

Charles had always been intrigued with wildlife, even so, finding the tones of the narrator's voice soporific, he had dozed off.

Awakened by a noise, bleary-eyed, he sat up. A dream or a reality? There it was again. The noise took the form of a howl. A howl of pain, or was it anguish?

Mary, in the doorway, her grey hair wet and dishevelled, her face ashen and expressionless, seemed lost for words. Something must have happened, but what?

'What's up?' Charles cried, a chill going down his spine. 'For heaven's sake tell me!'

'It's Marjorie, 'er's, 'er's ...' Mary, to his horror, collapsing on the floor, wept openly.

At that moment, the same howl issued from the set, that of a wolf on a rock, raising its head to the sky.

Charles, drawn by an inexplicable, uncanny feeling, glanced at the screen and then at Mary.

Chapter 7

'You do as I say, or else I'll cuff you across the ears. You're not too old for that and it might even knock some sense into you!'

Malcolm, having boarded the bus, had had other things on his mind up until then. Shaken out of his reverie, his curiosity aroused, he glanced in the direction of the speaker.

A dark-haired girl about Marjorie's age with, presumably, her brother from the way she was addressing him, were sitting just across the aisle. The boy, aged about eleven or twelve years old, dark-haired like his sister, his shoulders hunched, was looking decidedly glum.

'Well aren't you going to say anything, or are you just going to sit there and sulk?'

'But Sis, 'ow wos I to know 'e'd ride it? I wish I never …' he buried his head in his hands.

'James, time and time again I've warned you, haven't I … well, haven't I?'

Dumbstruck, James raised his head.

'What's the matter with you! Has the cat got your tongue?'

'Yes … I mean, no,' confused, James, fell silent.

'Harry Jenkins is trouble, with a capital T.' She was well and truly on her warhorse.

After a while, there was a lull in the conversation, brother and sister sitting in a subdued silence; the boy, having assumed his former glum expression, sat staring into space whilst his sister leafed through a magazine.

In the ensuing silence, and detached from the general hubbub, Malcolm reflected.

Only a week ago his life had been predictably dull, but it had taken a turn for the better since meeting Marjorie. His short association with her had added colour to an otherwise mundane existence. Her fresh approach to life had temporarily stimulated him and helped restore his faith in human nature.

His association with women up until now had been a disaster. Twenty-four years old, an only son, with his parents now living abroad with little or no contact: he hadn't missed them. He thought of them as cold, distant and aloof; he had envied those at university who, unlike him, came from a warm, loving background. On his own, he was living in a rented flat on the outskirts of Stonebridge. Having found a job, he now paid his way and wasn't answerable to anyone.

At university, where he had been studying for a degree in agriculture, he didn't take any of the girls seriously. He had played the field – that is until he met and become attracted to Natalie. With her black hair and blue eyes, he had become infatuated with her, as he had thought she was with him. Unbeknown to him, she had a string of admirers. This, he was to find to his cost when out of the blue she had announced that she was pregnant and that the child was his.

One evening, on turning up unexpectedly, he found the door to the flat open and he'd heard voices.

'How am I to know whose it is?' Natalie was saying. 'Does it matter? As long as the child has a father. Malcolm will do, even if he is as dull as ditch water.'

'Natalie, how could you?' Her friend had doubled up with laughter.

'So I'm dull, am I? Maybe, but I'm not a fool,' he cried, flinging the door wide open. 'Good job I found out before it was too late!'

He left them dumbstruck. Much to the consternation of his tutors, he abandoned his studies and returned home, only to find his parents had decided to sell up and live abroad on an impulse. In one fell swoop, the life he had known and counted on had become meaningless.

The high-pitched sound of a siren, the bus giving access to an ambulance speeding by, reminded him of the accident that had changed his life.

In his mind's eye, he again saw and experienced the treacherous road conditions, over which he had ridden with every fibre of his being. The panic had blurred his vision and dulled his senses; the accident was as if in slow motion with indistinct figures and muted voices. The bike was a crumpled heap of twisted metal. Shaken and shocked, he'd staggered to his feet. Helped to an ambulance, bleeding and sore, he'd wanted to know what had happened to Marjorie. The ambulance men's responses vague, he had been left thinking the worse.

Even now, after having been discharged as fit, he did not know what to expect on this, his first visit to the hospital since the tragedy. Obviously, Marjorie was alive, but how much alive? The hospital authorities were singularly unhelpful, because in their opinion, unrelated, he had no right to know. But yet, surely he had a right, for wasn't he partially responsible for the accident?

Chapter 8

Mary, finding the wheelchair heavy and cumbersome, stopped to mop her forehead with a pocket handkerchief. The hospital gates seemed a million miles away to her at that moment. Never one for giving up, she released the brake and carried on.

She had no idea how Charles was feeling, for since the accident, he had remained aloof, keeping himself to himself. He'd said very little, not even complained – this she had found odd and uncharacteristic. He had even taken to wearing dark glasses; she hadn't dared to ask why.

Apart from her mother's support, Mary now led a solitary existence. She was beginning to miss Charles' tantrums and demanding ways. His behaviour out of character, she almost wished he would swear at the television, or smash a dish as he had on one occasion, with Tibby refusing to go near him after a near miss. To fill this vacuum, now more than ever, she focused on the work in hand, irrespective of Charles' indifference.

Now and then, the vicar, Jeremiah Makepiece, or a member of the congregation of The Good Shepherd called to see her to offer any help and support. Touched by their kindness, she always refused any assistance, as a matter of pride. On one unforgettable visit, to her delight, a "get well soon" card for Marjorie, signed by members of the church, including Jeremiah, was delivered to her. A constant reminder, it now stood in pride of place on the television in the front room. So many happenings, so many people … had it only been three weeks since the accident? It had seemed a lifetime to Mary.

*

'Excuse me, my name is Malcolm Knight. I'm making an enquiry about a Miss Marjorie Henderson, brought in three weeks ago after a road accident.'

'Are you related?' The receptionist raised a pencilled eyebrow.

'No, but I too was involved in the accident. I was the rider; Miss Henderson was my pillion passenger.'

'In that case, wait here please.' Her manner brusque, she promptly disappeared.

*

Mary, sitting in the foyer with Charles now dozing in his wheel-chair, had overheard the conversation. ''E be Malcolm,' she mouthed. 'So that's what 'e looks like.' She eyed him critically. They had never met him, but had spoken on the telephone on several occasions before the accident.

On the surface, he seemed a nice enough young man, although rather older than she'd imagined, maybe a little too old for Marjorie, but he had a pleasant face and nice manners. Aware of her interest, he smiled before turning away.

'I'm afraid we cannot reveal any information about the patient, that is unless you are a relation.' The receptionist with the pencilled eyebrows was back.

Malcolm's face fell.

Mary, putting two and two together, with Charles still asleep and Malcolm about to leave, got up to stop him. 'Wait, don't go,' she cried, 'I be Mary, Marj's Ma. 'E must be Malcolm, 'er friend from work.'

Malcolm, stopping in his tracks, studied her face. 'I would never have known it was you, but I recognize your voice,' he said. His brow furrowed. 'I suppose you wouldn't know how she is? I've been imagining all sorts of things.'

Mary could do nothing but empathise – she patted him on the arm. And in a low tone of voice, said, 'Our Marj is in a coma … it be touch an' go.'

'Oh, my God! It's worse than I thought.' He stared unbelievingly into space. 'I blame myself!' With a suspicion of a tear, Malcolm turned away, as if unable to come to terms with the situation.

'Don't 'e fret, it ain't your fault. T'was an accident with a dog, 'e won't to know.' Mary, seeing how devastated he was, sharpening her tone, thought up ways to soften the blow. 'If 'e has time, why don' 'e come home with me an' Charles. Us could 'ave a chat an' a cup of tea.'

*

Malcolm insisted on pushing the wheelchair. Charles, awake, now wanted to know who he was. Was he a male nurse?

Malcolm, Mary told him, had been with Marjorie at the time of the accident and was the rider of the bike of which she had been the pillion passenger.

Charles, angered by her remark, at last breaking his sustained silence, shouted, ''E's not pushin' me!'

'Charles, stop making a fool of yerself, folks are lookin'!' Mary, acutely aware of a number of faces turning their way, blushed.

'Let 'em look!' he firmed his lips.''Ain't they got nothin' better to do?'

'Quiet!' Mary raised her voice. 'I've had enough of 'e an' yer hullabaloo, tis 'bout time 'e grew up.' Even so, in her heart of hearts, the silence broken, she was relieved to think Charles was communicating again.

Malcolm, on the other hand, embarrassed by the incident and uncertain what to do, suggested that they meet up another time.

'Nothing of the sort!' Mary exclaimed. 'I ain't going to pander to 'im.'

With a growing tiredness, relieved to have Malcolm's support and company, she didn't want to lose him.

*

'Make yerself at 'ome.' Mary pulled out a chair for Malcolm then set about making the tea.

Charles, in his wheelchair by the range, feigning sleep, closed his eyes.

'I thought us could 'ave it in 'ere,' she said, ''Tis cosy with the range. Us stokes it up in winter, or with a run of bad weather. Tis 'bout time to put the kettle on.'

Mary, reaching for the cake tin, aware of being watched by Malcolm, felt a headache coming on. Something was worrying her, but what? She searched her mind. A thought occurred. Tibby, where was Tibby? She had completely neglected her.

'The cat, it ain't been fed,' she cried. ''Er must 'ave gone off somewhere, 'er … must be found, tis Marj's.'

Malcolm, mustering up a smile, nodded.

In the back garden, calling her name, Mary found no response, not a sign. Tibby must be found. As she stood, waiting in anticipation, she pondered, wherever was Tibby and why was Charles so antagonistic towards Malcolm? The accident had been a shock and a severe blow in itself for all of them, but there was something about Charles' attitude, something she couldn't fathom.

Chapter 9

Wednesday, Pam Jenkins' day off, found her ensconced in her favourite armchair with a box of Quality Street. A romantic at heart, she was absorbed in her favourite Mills & Boon paperback.

Life hadn't always been so easy-going in the early years of her marriage. Robert, just like his brother, Patrick, was endowed with a restless nature – he had had problems settling down. At that time, on leaving the Royal Navy, he had experienced a certain amount of difficulty in adapting to civilian life and finding suitable employment. With Oliver a toddler, Harry on the way and Robert, frustrated and bored, hanging around the house, her nerves at times had been at breaking point. She dreaded the times when Patrick was home on leave from the Merchant Navy. Single and fancy free, she considered him a bad influence, an added problem to an already difficult situation. The brothers would go out on a pub crawl, coming home in the small hours drunk and incapable, sometimes with a police escort and a warning.

At times, there had seemed no light at the end of the tunnel until one evening, on one of his frequent visits, Robert chanced to meet up with an old schoolmate who persuaded him to join in a business venture. Ted's steadying influence, although at first suspect, had proved to be Robert's saving grace. Robert's attending night school with a view to becoming a landscape gardener had paid off. Now, with Ted as a partner, the small business was a veritable gold mine. Not wanting to employ extra staff, the two men worked long hours and were always in demand.

Pam was proud of Oliver, her eldest, too. Tall, dark-haired and similar in looks to Robert, like her and his father, Oliver was fired with ambition and a desire to get on. He was an achiever and it had come as no surprise when he had been accepted for a university course. Robert, too, hoped in time that he would be able to include Oliver in the business, with a view to handing over his share when necessary. So Pam's world was complete, but for Harry …

Although Patrick now rarely appeared on the scene, when he did, Pam worried. Harry was a manifestation of Uncle Patrick, having inherited his red hair, fiery temper and wild ways. Aimless and critical of Oliver, he rebelled and refused any advice, seemingly bent on destroying the family's respectable middle-class image. He had become secretive and abusive if questioned. Pam was worried – had he, like Uncle Patrick, turned to drink? On various occasions, she had found half-empty bottles in the drink cabinet. She had no idea what Harry was doing half the time. For with Robert's long hours and her full-time job as a hairdresser, there didn't seem to be enough hours in the day to find out.

Pam, coming to the end of the chapter, having ear-marked her place, closed the paperback. She prised herself out of the chair and, stepping over to the window, looked out. It was a grey and overcast day, with a tendency to drizzle, and it probably would stay that way – not her sort of day. She crossed the room to study her face in the mirror over the mantelpiece: with only fine lines on her forehead, a slight frown mark and hardly any crow's feet, her hair still the colour of ripe corn with a little help from a bottle, she had worn well. Her blue eyes in response gazed back at her as if in acknowledgement. Memories of that day so long ago came into her mind – her wedding day, with church bells ringing, of smiling, happy faces and showers of confetti, the look of love in Robert's eyes as he looked into hers. So much water had gone under the bridge, but then was then, and now was now, and where was Harry?

Pam, stepping to the window, glanced out. The street was damp. There was a misty rain, but there was no sign of Harry, only that of a solitary milk float ponderously making its way homeward, its headlights casting shafts of golden light across the gravely grey surfaces of the road. The day, she thought, was coming to a close, and with it the darkness. A wind picking up, the street lights would soon cast their glow. Somewhere a dog howled. For some unaccountable reason, she shivered.

She switched on a newly acquired art deco lamp and before drawing the curtains, an overhead light. Time to spare, she questioned, her eyes fixed on the settee, for another cup of coffee before tea and a chapter of her paperback?

It was an afternoon such as this, only a week ago, that coming home unexpectedly, she found Harry sprawled on the settee, sound asleep, with a small package on a nearby table. On closer inspection, it revealed a substance. Disturbed by her close proximity, Harry, rolling over, muttered in his sleep. Pam, leaning over him, had managed to catch the words, 'The dog … it's getting closer! It's …' Harry, waking up, perspiring and fearful, had sat up. 'It ain't nothing,' he'd said, pocketing the package, the moment having passed. Needless to say, the episode still preyed on Pam's mind. She hated inactivity and unsolvable problems.

She'd despaired when informed of Marjorie's accident and later she was mortified by the severity of the injury, which by its very nature had rendered her helpless. Mary, so proud, could only give emotional support and promise to stay in touch. The sight of Harry mooning about the house, with no apparent interest in anything didn't help and she was glad when he went out.

Now she felt guilty. Where was he? Was it partly her fault, should she shoulder some of the blame?

She'd stubbed out her cigarette and drained the remains of her coffee and was just picking up her paperback when the telephone rang. *Who on earth can it be?* she asked herself while lifting the receiver. It was Oliver.

'How lovely to hear from you, how are you?'

'Fine thanks.'

'I was going to ring you tonight.' She hesitated. 'Prepare yourself; I'm afraid I'm the bearer of bad news.'

'Oh?'

'Marjorie Henderson's in a coma.' Her words came out in a rush.

'What!' A long, drawn-out silence prevailed.

'Oliver, are you still there?' Pat jiggled the cradle

'Yes, I heard you … Are you sure?'

'Of course I'm sure! Harry was riding your Honda.'

'What? My bike! Oh no, not my bike, I'll kill him! I thought I'd locked up the shed before I went away. How did he start it without a key?'

'The key was in the ignition.'

'I've been looking for it everywhere, so that's where it was!'

'He's very upset.'

'So he should be … can I speak to him?'

'He isn't here, he's gone out. He won't speak to me. I feel so guilty.'

'You, guilty! You and Dad did all you could to put him on the straight and narrow, but he just didn't want to know. But Marjorie, I don't understand …'

'Marjorie was riding pillion on a scooter, with a young man who had offered her a lift home from her job at a gardening centre. Harry, you know how wild he can be, had taken it into his head to ride your bike. He's always had a crush on her, and seeing them together, he took chase, until the dog …'

'What dog?'

'It's a stray dog that doesn't trust anyone. It hangs around the streets and is unapproachable. The accident happened three weeks ago. Earlier in the day there had been a thick, misty rain and low cloud, giving way to clear visibility; the roads were still wet and treacherous. The dog, without warning, suddenly leapt out as if from nowhere.'

'What happened to it?'

'No one knows.'

'And Harry?'

'Strong as an ox, our Harry is, he simply got up and walked away with just a few scratches and minor injuries.'

'The bike?'

'Damaged, but can be repaired, so we've been told.'

'I could wring his neck! The other guy, was he hurt?'

'I believe his name is Malcolm Knight. Miraculously, he

escaped with only superficial injuries, but was in shock and had to be sedated.'

'That's funny, the name rings a bell. I think I remember hearing something about him, but I can't remember for the life of me what it was.'

'Try to remember.'

'I'll do my best. I've got to go, there's someone tapping on the glass. If I come up with anything I'll let you know. My heart goes out to Marjorie's parents. Tell Harry I'll be expecting a phone call.'

*

Pam, glancing at the clock, set aside her paperback for another day. Time had flown. In the kitchen, having placed a home-made pie in the oven, she laid the table for tea. The serenity of the moment was broken by a rumble of thunder; a storm was approaching. In the lounge, she drew back the curtains. A sheet of lightning flashed across her vision, followed by a loud clap of thunder, and then, as if the Earth held its breath, it exhaled, unleashing a tremendous downpour. She switched off the light, marvelling at the power and beauty of nature, as yet another flash of lightning lit the darkened room. The spell was broken with a persistent knocking at the door.

She turned on the light and hurried into the hall. She opened the front door. Heavy rain borne on a gust of wind temporarily blinding her, she could only make out two shapes in an inky, black darkness. The shapes, having manifested themselves outside on the step, wet and bedraggled and out of breath, she saw as Ruby, clutching her brother, James', hand.

'Whatever are you doing out in this weather?' Pam exclaimed. 'For goodness sake, come in and dry off; you'll both catch your death of cold.' She took some towels from an airing cupboard and handed them over, saying, 'Rub yourselves down.'

'We're alright, really.' Ruby indicated James was dripping water on the hall carpet. His face pallid, his lower lip trembling, he shifted his feet from side to side in nervous anticipation.

'You look worried, son, what's the matter?'

'Speak up, for heaven's sake. I'm fast beginning to lose patience with you.' Ruby, pushing James towards Pam, exclaimed, 'Tell her what you were going to tell Harry!'

'Well, it's ... it's just ...'

'Yes?' prompted Pam, mustering up a smile.

'That I feel, I ...' then with a rush of words, 'talked 'Arry into it.'

'You!' Pam exclaimed.

'Harry wouldn'a thought of riding the bike if it 'adn't been fer me. 'E was just showing me it.'

'Don't you fret on that score, he would have in his own good time ... you don't know our Harry.' Pam ruffled James' hair. 'Now you run off home and forget it ever happened, there's a good lad.'

James, humiliated, smiled a weak smile. Ruby, having thanked Pam profusely, propelled him down the garden path.

Pam, standing at the door, watched them go and sighed. What a day off – not a moment's peace. Robert should be home any minute. And the pie, she had forgotten the pie! The kitchen full of smoke, she opened the window, coughing. In the hall the telephone rang. Robert working overtime? She would soon know. But it wasn't Robert, it was Harry.

'Harry, where are you? Whatever are you doing out in this weather? Will you be coming home for tea?'

'I've bin doing nothin' ... I ain't coming 'ome, ever again.''

'But Harry ... why?'

There was no reply. The line went dead. She stood there for a moment, and then, stepping into the lounge, she shut the door. Not knowing or caring, she had come to the end of her tether.

*

Harry, soaked to the skin, dodged rapidly forming puddles – seepage from the surrounding fields soon turning the narrow lane into a quagmire. A passing car travelling at speed, sending up a cascade of water in its wake, prompted him to shout back expletives.

Down in the dumps, he plodded on, but not aimlessly, for he was making his way to the railway station. Not far away, just a few miles from the outskirts of Stonebridge. He would soon be there.

He had sufficient money; his mother's money, a recent wage packet containing a month's salary, the like of which she had been intending to pay into the savings bank for safekeeping. With this thought in mind, when fingering the packet, he experienced an unusual spasm of guilt, an emotion he generally dismissed as a weakness. He resolved himself, and without a care in the world, he carried on his way, with a view to reaching the main road where he would thumb a lift.

Up until now, Harry hadn't thought much about the accident, and when by chance he did, he blanked it out, choosing not to dwell on it. For whenever he truly thought about it, of his part in it, and its devastating effect on Marjorie and the damage to his brother's bike, he knew he'd crossed the line – that this time there would be no turning back. Without a doubt, the best thing to do was to 'up sticks' and go, join the Merchant Navy like Uncle Patrick, to find a new life.

But what about the nightmares that came and went at will? The darkness, pitch black, then suddenly and much more frightening, a howl, as if of an animal in pain. The sound taking the form of a dog's face at first, indistinct and then well defined, slowly fading, then changing to that of a human's, soon without shape or substance.

If he told anyone, who would believe him? They would say he was making it up. Harry, at his wit's end, had turned to drink and, more recently, to drugs.

As rounding a bend in the lane, a pathetic mew drew his attention. The misty rain having eased, a watery moon lit up the narrow lane revealing a wet bundle of fur, caught up in a nearby thicket. On closer inspection, it disclosed a cat, vainly attempting to disentangle itself from its wayside prison.

Harry's first reaction was to ignore the creature and leave it to its fate, but the mews, demanding and pitiful, grew louder. He stopped to investigate. On his approach, the cat, for a moment, stopped struggling. It eyed him suspiciously, then, struggling again, only succeeded in making the situation worse. Weakened by its activities, it allowed Harry to free it. Free at last, it walked gingerly down the lane to disappear through a farm gate.

Harry, although puzzled by his undue concern for the cat, went on his way. Some way to go yet, but worth it in the long run, he thought.

'But what is that?' he exclaimed, on hearing a persistent mewing.

Choosing to ignore it, he trudged on, the cat padding not far behind him. Exasperated by its unexpected appearance, he picked up some pebbles and threw them at it. Undeterred, it continued shadowing him, the gap narrowing.

Harry, maddened by the creature's persistence, tried every-thing he could think of to get rid of it, from throwing pebbles, shouting and ignoring it, but all to no avail. The cat seemed to have nine lives, for even on the main road, he had been aware of it. No way was it going to give up its endless pursuit.

At last, the journey at an end, the railway station, its lights beckoning, loomed up ahead. Harry breathed a sigh of relief. No one had offered him a lift – tired and irritable, his legs like lead on reaching his destination, his mother's wage packet was the only consolation.

Purposely joining a small queue of people and pushing his way through the turnstile, he approached the kiosk, not once looking behind.

'Is it yours?' the ticket collector pointed his finger in the direction of the turnstile.

Harry, looking over his shoulder, saw to his dismay the cat sat just behind him, cleaning and preening itself, with not a care in the world.

'No 'er ain't, I don't want 'er, 'er thinks 'er is!' Harry by now had had enough. He glared at the cat. The cat held his gaze, much to the amusement of the people in the queue.

'Well, here's yer ticket; make sure it doesn't follow 'e onto the train.'

Moments later, Harry, standing on the platform, watched an incoming train shunting into the station. The place a hive activity, Harry, mesmerised, stood watching people coming and going. Aware of a presence, he looked back. The cat, sitting at a distance, was staring at him intently.

'Well, lad, make up yer mind, will 'e be boardin' the train or no?' a gruff voice, that of a guard, distracted him.

Harry didn't know what to say. Now the time had come to "up sticks" like Uncle Patrick, he wasn't so sure. Why was that? Was he losing his nerve? Puzzled, he looked at the cat. It held his gaze.

'Speak up!'

Harry, having made up his mind, shook his head.

'Suit yerself, son, us 'aven't got all night.'

Harry watched the train vanishing into the tunnel, taking with it his bid for freedom. He could only feel a sense of relief.

The cat, in the same place, was still staring at him. Aware of his interest, getting up, it approached him, purring, and encircled his legs.

Harry, completely out of character, bent down and stroked its furry head.

The cat had become a friend. With the cat he could be himself. The animal's persistence had paid off. No longer lonely or uncertain, to him, at that moment, it offered a kind of love, a kind of affection with no strings attached. It filled an emotional need, a need sorely lacking in his life.

On leaving the station, the cat, as if by instinct, determined the way. Harry followed as if in a dream, not knowing nor caring why, across roads, down lanes, even fields, moving away from the outskirts into the market town.

The cat, suddenly stopping outside a cottage, padded up the garden path and scratched on the front door.

The cottage was in darkness. True to its nature, the cat persisted. Lights coming on, the door opened, revealing the outline of a figure. Harry, having taken refuge in the shrubbery, saw a woman in a dressing gown, her hair in curlers, standing in the doorway, rubbing her eyes.

On seeing the cat, she dropped to her knees, fondling it, she cried, 'Charles, Tibby's come 'ome.'

A murmured response issued from within, something like, 'Wot's 'e doing out of bed.' Don't 'e worry 'bout 'er.' With that, she picked up the cat. Closing the door, she turned out the lights, leaving the cottage in darkness.

Harry, parting the leaves concealing his hiding place, clambered out. The moon emerging from behind a cloud, silvering the landscape, he took to the road.

Chapter 10

Malcolm, alighting from the bus, walked the short distance to the flat. All was quiet; Mrs Piper must be out.

The sun was receding behind the clouds, in its place an enhancing glow, indicating the passing of a warm summer's day; even so, Malcolm shivered as he rummaged for the key.

Malcolm, finding the atmosphere in the flat oppressive, having contained the heat of the day, unlatched the window. For a while he stood by the sill, breathing in the balmy air. It had been a disheartening day: things had not gone to plan, and as for Marjorie, he was none the wiser. Weary, dumping his haversack on the floor, he slumped into the nearest chair.

Earlier, in Charles' presence, he had felt very much on guard. To be fair, Charles, true to his word, had not prolonged his verbal assault, but sat there quietly scrutinizing him, thus creating an uneasy atmosphere, one from which he longed to be free. Obviously, Charles had every right to be upset, but hadn't Mary too? With neither of them knowing how to deal with a situation that was becoming increasingly difficult? Somewhat relieved when taking his leave, he had promised to keep in touch.

He slipped out of his jacket, and pulling on a pair of comfy mules, he filled the kettle with water. In the kitchen annexe, having lit the gas, he placed it on the portable stove. The biscuit tin on the shelf above contained only one or two broken digestives and a few crumbs – another item, he thought, to remember for the shopping list.

As cupping the mug in his hands, savouring and taking comfort from its warming contents, he thought of his evening meal. A pie purchased on the spur of the moment, not too crumbly – too much to eat? Fish and chips, now there's a thought. A creak of the staircase and a brief knock, with a scrap of paper pushed under the door, broke a train of thought that juggled the supper alternatives.

A short note scribbled in a familiar hand, read: "Didn't want to disturb you, you hadn't collected your mail from the hall table, so I've left it outside the door. L. Piper."

Malcolm, sifting through the pile, found junk mail, a letter from his parents, an overdue gas bill and more junk mail. He put the gas bill in the urgent file, then slit open and proceeded to read the letter from his parents.

So his parents were settling down and adjusting to their new life in Spain, were they? A footnote suggested he should pay them a visit. Not in a million years! *There's nothing in this for me! Better I got myself something to eat.* Malcolm, losing interest, tearing it and the junk mail into shreds, tossed the pieces into the waste bin.

In the kitchen, on the point of raiding the fridge, there was a loud knock on the door. He opened it to find a turbaned and aproned Mrs Piper standing outside.

'Yer wanted on the phone.'

'Who by?' he asked.

'I don't know, I never asked.'

Now who could that be? he wondered, following her down the stairs. *Hardly anybody rings me here.*

Still wondering, down in the dingy hallway, he picked up the mouthpiece. 'Hello.'

'Is that Malcolm Knight?'

'Speaking?'

'I don't know if you remember me. I'm Oliver Jenkins; we rubbed shoulders briefly at university.'

'Rubbed shoulders?' The voice seemed familiar. Malcolm, wracking his brain, drew a blank. 'I'm sorry, I've no recollection.'

For a short while, silence prevailed.

'Hello, hello … are you still there?'

'Yes, I'm still here. I wonder …' Again, a pause. 'Maybe we could meet somewhere?' The voice timorous, laced with uncertainty, tailed off.

'Why would you want to meet me?' The emphasis in Malcolm's reply, clearly on "me".

'It's because …'

'Yes?'

Silence.

'Hello, hello?' Malcolm raised his voice, with no response. 'Now who the devil was that?' he muttered. On lighting a cigarette, soothed by a lazy spiral of smoke, he stood for a while deep in thought before ascending the stairs.

*

'Marjorie, Marjorie!' he cried, his voice louder and persistent. 'It's Malcolm, I work with you at the garden centre.' He glanced out the window, at cedar trees swaying in the breeze, fringing the hospital car park. Another day, another visit, if, God willing, there would be an end to this nightmare and she would be back again where she belonged.

'We first met in the restaurant, don't you remember? I said, "May I share your table?" to which you replied, "My name's, Marjorie, I've just been taken on, I'm to work in the gift shop on Saturdays." It was a joke we shared … don't you remember? Marjorie, Marjorie … where are you now, why don't you answer me? Do you remember when first we met?'

The figure lying in the bed not responding, Malcolm moved a little closer. To him, Marjorie had never looked so beautiful. Her face serene and free from care, long silken lashes caressing her cheeks, her hair the colour of corn, she looked like an angel in repose, his angel. If only he had never given her a lift … if only this, if only that, in an ideal world, if only one could look into the future, take precautions.

The clock ticking; the relentless march of time.

The sun setting, a great ball of fire now sinking towards the horizon. In a moment or two its dying glow silhouetting nearby trees and distant countryside.

She stirred? Wishful thinking? He watched as shadows, deepening, chasing each other across the walls, filled the small room with imaginary images, some good, some bad. His mind playing tricks? The silence punctuated by her steady breathing, he glanced at the monitor, registering her heartbeats, a constant reminder of the fragility of life.

A ceiling fan stirred lazily as a gentle breeze wafted through the open window. Beside her bed were flowers, an assortment of get-well cards and a little pink teddy bear.

At that moment a nurse entered the room. Smiling at Malcolm, she gathered up the flowers, and placing them on a little trolley, wheeled them out of the room, dislodging the little bear in the process.

Alone again, Malcolm, overcome with curiosity, picked it up. On a tag attached to a bow tied around its neck, he read the words, "With all my love, dearest Marjorie, Tim." *Who was Tim?* he pondered. Could it be a boyfriend, one she hadn't told him about? Not that it was any of his business. Even so, he felt a wave of strong emotion, one of jealousy, anger or love? Which one? He couldn't tell. 'Don't be silly,' he muttered, inwardly admonishing himself, 'I'm wasting my time, she might not even like me in that way. I must try to think of something else.' He knew he must, it was the only way.

For this purpose he moved to the window and sat down, through the panes watching birds at dusk, winging home to their nests. Mary's face came to mind. Overburdened with grief, she'd grasped his hand in a last ditch attempt to get him to stay. Saddened by the sight, he had consoled her, tried to reassure her, watched by an impassive, wheelchair-bound, Charles.

The door opening broke his chain of thought; he looked up. A dark-haired girl was standing in the doorway, clutching the hand of a boy. The nurse with them, having shown them in, left abruptly.

Surprised by the sudden intrusion, Malcolm at first didn't know what to think. Their faces familiar, he could have sworn he'd seen them before, but where? He searched his mind but was none the wiser.

'I don't think we've met.' The girl, still standing by the door, nervously fidgeting, twisted an unruly strand of hair. 'I'm Ruby, and that's my brother, James.' She cast a sidelong glance at a boy, as quiet as a mouse.

Malcolm, feeling a modicum of pity, smiled at the boy, who didn't respond. Then turning to Ruby, said, 'You must be wondering who I am. I'm Malcolm; I'm a friend of Marjorie. I've only known her for a short time through working at the Oasis Garden Centre.'

'Oh,' Ruby, glancing at the little pink bear now propped up on the bedside cabinet, blushed. 'I didn't know what to bring under the circumstances.'

'Just yourselves, that will do,' Malcolm, studying her face, empathised.

'You didn't say how you knew Marjorie, but it's just come to me, I remember you. You were on the bus travelling into Stonebridge from the outskirts late one afternoon. I was sitting adjacent to you.'

By Ruby's side, James, glancing up at Malcolm, having caught his gaze, stared down at his feet.

'Oh, if we're in your way.'

'I didn't say that, did I?' Malcolm, drawing out some chairs, patted the seats. 'Sit down and tell me about yourselves.'

Ruby, taking up the offer, relaxed. James sat down beside her. 'There's nothing really to tell, Marjorie and I have been friends as long as I can remember. And like me, in her last year at school. That is, until she got the job.'

'And James?'

'Oh him!' Ruby, glad to be free of Malcolm's scrutiny, cast a disdainful eye at her brother. 'He's a menace!'

'I ain't!' James retorted.

'I'm not,' reprimanded Ruby, 'talk proper; you're getting just like Harry.'

'Who's Harry?'

'James' friend. He's a bad lot, so Ma says. It's his fault isn't it? It would never have happened if it wasn't for him.' Ruby eyed Malcolm, fully expecting him to agree.

'What?' Malcolm had no idea what she was talking about.

'The accident; he shouldn't have been riding the bike.' She squeezed James' hand. 'He thinks it's his fault, you know, but it isn't.'

''Tis,' said James, suddenly finding his tongue, ''cos I talked 'im into it.'

'It is, not 'tis,' exclaimed the ever vigilant Ruby, 'and it's because, not 'cos.'

James, shrugging his shoulders, subsided into a sulky silence.

An attitude of no significance, for Malcolm, fired by a thought, was beginning to see the light.

'So Harry was the motorcyclist.'

Still exasperated with James behaviour, Ruby at first didn't reply, and then, 'Harry, the motorcyclist? Yes, didn't you know, I thought everyone did.'

'Where is he now?' Malcolm, somewhat annoyed at having been kept in the dark, wanted to know more.

'I … we don't know.' Ruby, flustered and ill at ease, wondered what was expected of her.

At that moment, they became aware of the hurried sound of footsteps, that of a nurse, who the very next moment would tell them it was time to go.

Ruby, somewhat relieved, made her way to the door, where beckoning to her brother, she said, 'Come on James, we'll be late for tea.' She glanced back at Malcolm, and smiling nervously, commented, 'It's been nice meeting you.'

'Yes, very nice.' Malcolm, standing in the doorway, watched them descend the stairs two at a time. 'Yes,' he muttered, 'very nice, nicer than you know.'

Chapter 11

'Do 'e want me to wash or wipe, dear?' Amelia pointed to a stack of dishes.

Her daughter, drawing on her apron, apparently deep in thought, didn't respond.

'Did 'e 'ear me, what I said?

Mary, still pre-occupied, responded half-heartily, 'What is it, Ma? What's wrong?'

'Nothing, shall I wash or wipe?'

'Oh, the dishes. Really Ma, I never bothers to wipe 'em nowadays; just leaves 'em to dry on the draining board.'

Mary, picking up the washing liquid, squirted some into a bowl. She drew on a pair of rubber gloves and equipped with a pad, proceeded to soak and rinse the dishes.

'Let me 'ave a go,' Amelia said, moving towards her, hands outstretched.

'No, leave it!' Mary, acutely aware of Amelia's reaction to her rebuff, suggested, 'If 'e wants to be useful, put the kettle on. I'm thirsty; I'm gagging fer a cup of tea.'

Amelia, with a pang, filling the kettle, glanced at her daughter. Mary, standing at the kitchen sink, looked almost twice her age. Shoulders hunched, wayward tendrils of grey hair hanging down, frequently pushed back from a careworn face – she stood with sleeves rolled up, intent on her task. A picture of a figure resigned to suffering.

'Tea's made, shall I take it in?' Amelia, intent on lightening her load, added, 'I've brought 'e some biscuits, yer favourites.'

'Thanks, Ma.'

At that moment, nudging open the kitchen door, Tibby came in. As usual, making a beeline for Mary, purring, she encircled her legs.

Mary, managing a smile, bent down to smooth her silky fur.

'It's nice to 'ave 'er back, Charles thought I was making a lot of fuss 'bout nothing.'

'Where is 'e, anyway?' Amelia raised an eyebrow. 'It don't seem the same without 'im, by the range.'

'In the front room having 'is afternoon nap, 'e won't want any tea. On second thoughts, us won't want to wake 'im, 'tis best us 'aves ours in the kitchen.'

'Come sit yourself down,' Amelia patted the nearest chair, 'let's 'ave a chat.'

'I don't know what I'd do without 'e, Ma.' Mary at that moment felt like a weight had been lifted off her shoulders.

'What are mother's fer?'

Amelia, settling back in her chair, sipped her tea. 'Tell me,' she said, as replacing the cup in its saucer, 'ave 'e heard anything more 'bout Harry?'

'No, though Pam rings every day to ask 'bout Marj. Suppose 'er feels awkward, with 'Arry an' all.'

Amelia nodded her head. 'The lad must be a constant worry, 'e takes after 'is uncle, so I've been told. There's always one bad apple in the barrel, ain't there?' Changing the subject, Amelia said, 'Tell me 'bout Marjie's young man.'

''E's hardly young, 'e's several years older than Marj. An' 'er's only known 'im fer a short time. He's a nice enough lad. Pam tells me Oliver knew 'im at university, that 'e harbours secrets, you know, keeps things to he-self.'

Intrigued, Amelia asked, 'Where do 'e live?'

'On the outskirts in a flat, 'is parents being out in Spain.'

'So 'e's all on 'is own?'

Mary nodded. 'So it seems. 'E visits Marj regular an' helps out with Charles.'

'How's Charles?'

'He's not the same. Struck dumb, 'e says nothing since the accident, it's as if …' Mary, pausing, frowned, clasping and unclasping her hands, she seemed lost for words.

'Yes?' Amelia raised an enquiring eyebrow.

'As if 'e's afraid of …'

'Yes?'

'Doesn't matter. Let's forget …' she hadn't finished the sentence when …

'Mary, Mary! … where's me tea?' a loud and demanding voice broke the silence.

'Speak of the devil, 'e's awake, I'll have to make 'im a fresh cuppa.'

'Let me.' Amelia, rising to her feet, put the kettle on.

Minutes later, the tea brewed, she carried in the tray, followed by Tibby.

'Git that cat out of me sight,' Charles, by the window, glared.

Tibby, objecting to his angry tone of voice, made for the door.

'Here's yer tea, Charles,' Amelia, speaking in a soft tone, tried to act as if nothing had happened.

Charles, grunting in response, picking up a newspaper, pretended to be absorbed in it, the tea lying untouched on a nearby table.

Amelia, back in the kitchen, found Mary sitting at the table, her head in her hands. Her heart bled at the sight. 'Try not to let it get 'e down.'

She placed a hand on her arm and Mary, raising her head, buried it momentarily against the warmth of her mother's breast, saying in a muffled tone, 'Do 'e think Marj will ever come out of this … will us ever be back to a normal way of life? Oh, Ma, I dread to think what might 'appen. If only …' she paused, her face crumbling, as succumbing to tears.

'Why don't 'e go and lie down, I'll see to 'im.' Amelia, wiping the tear-stained face and smoothing the unruly hair, saw Mary as a child again, just as she would have been then, vulnerable and afraid.

'Thanks Ma; that I will.' Mary, managing a wan smile, squeezed her mother's hand before ascending the stairs.

Amelia, toying with a cup of lukewarm tea and a half-eaten biscuit, pondered. Who would have thought this time last year, what a well of despondency they would find themselves in –

no one ever knew what was around the corner. At that moment Tibby, on reappearing, prowled around the room, mewing plaintively.

'Do 'e want to go out?' Amelia, opening the back door, gestured persuasively to no avail. Tibby, continuing to prowl in an agitated manner, clawed the carpet, as if registering some sort of protest. Finally coming to rest, sitting on her haunches, her green eyes narrowing to slits, she fixed them on Amelia, as if trying to communicate.

An experience she found very disconcerting.

Apart from Tibby's restlessness, elsewhere with no movement, one could hear a pin drop.

I'll see to Charles, she thought, eager for some sort of diversion.

She found him sitting in his customary place by the window. He was staring fixedly at something. Something she couldn't see.

Not moving a muscle, he remained in a trance-like state.

Unnerved by the situation, Amelia wondered what to do next. She didn't want to involve Mary, particularly now.

She clapped her hands, exclaiming, 'Charles, Charles, wake up!' There was no response.

Then a movement. Charles turned and looked in her direction, but he wasn't looking at her. At that moment Tibby, having followed her in, arched her back, flattened her ears and with a waving tail, held his stare. From her throat issued a hissing, almost sinister sound.

Charles, as if in response and to Amelia's horror, started to howl, an unearthly sound, a sound filling her with dread. She wanted to run away, but riveted to the spot, could only stand and stare.

Aware of a presence, she looked over her shoulder to see Mary. She was standing half-dressed in the doorway. Horror-stricken, she cried, 'Ring fer the doctor. Wot's happenin'? Oh my God!'

Chapter 12

The sun was setting as Jeremiah Makepiece purposely rode his bicycle up the lane to the church, where as a welcomed spectator he was hoping to spend an hour or two, listening to the Saturday-night choir practice. Saddle sore, a little way on, he got off, wheeling his bike. He walked the rest of the way. On reaching the lychgate, he saw a dog sprawled on a grassy knoll. A fearsome creature, it eyed him with contempt. Never one to tempt providence, he decided to leave it to its own devices.

Having reached the church, he propped his bike against the wall, to find, on entering the porch, the heavy oaken door inside ajar. He had in the past left the church unlocked for the benefit of his parishioners, but lately due to the onset of darker evenings, tended to lock it. The door creaking as pushing it, he stepped inside into the quiet, dim interior.

He always enjoyed the quiet, for it was at times like this, inspired by God's presence, seated at his desk in the vestry, he'd sometimes compile his forthcoming Sunday sermon.

On entering such hallowed surroundings, he knelt down and prayed as usual. Prayers for his parents; the deceased, that they may rest in peace; for the world with its trials and tribulations; for Marjorie, still in a coma; for Emma Wescott, the grocer's wife, who had fallen down the stairs and damaged her back; for Erica Johnson, permanently on the sick list. Finally making the sign of the cross, rising to his feet, he sat for a time in one of the bench-like pews, drinking in the atmosphere. A few minutes later, a sound of voices, an echo of approaching feet on concrete, the clunk of the latch and the creaking of the heavy door swinging open, admitting, in person, familiar faces – those of the choir.

*

Harry, disturbed by the sound of organ music reverberating

around the church, awoke with a start. At first, drowsy and still half asleep, he thought himself in heaven. A stone angel smiling benignly down at him from one of the pillars as he lay full length on a pew almost convinced him, but he soon realised, he wasn't. He was hungry, dirty and on the run.

Intrigued by melodious renderings and taking care not to be seen, he propped himself up sufficiently to look over the back of the pew in front. A shaft of light from a stained-glass window, throwing out multi-coloured patterns, picked out and highlighted the vicar. He was sitting in a pew at the front of the church, listening to a group of people, both male and female, some as young as himself. At this time, as watching from his vantage point with pangs of hunger gnawing at his stomach, Harry, who had always avoided baths, longed to have one. Only yesterday, when purchasing sandwiches, fruit and soft drinks with his dwindling amount of money, he had been acutely aware of the shopkeeper's disgust when taking and pocketing his change with a grimy hand.

Harry, tiring of his current way of life, contemplated his next move. If it hadn't been for the cat and the strange effect it had had on him, having boarded the train by now, he would have been miles away, leaving Stonebridge and all his problems behind him. Now all he longed for was a hot bath and the comfort of a warm bed, preferably at home. He had no illusions about his reception there. Although in the past he had been able to get around his mother, this time, even as far as she was concerned, he had crossed the line. He shuddered when he thought of his father's reaction. He must act now.

Keeping a low profile he crawled noiselessly, Red Indian style, along the length of the bench, at the end of which he peered nervously around the corner, finding to his relief the vicar still preoccupied. Although the bench was adjacent to the church door, it seemed to him a million miles away. When crawling he stopped only once to check all was well. Fortunately, the church door being slightly ajar enabled him to prise it open, albeit the slightest creak filled him with alarm. With the expertise of a commando on manoeuvres, he soon found himself outside the door, his extremities in contact with the cold flagstone of the porch. He shivered as a cool breeze wafted in from the darkened churchyard, from a cold, crisp night, velvet black, pinpointed with innumerable stars, a full moon casting its silvery glow, here and there eerie shadows dancing amid tombstones and long grasses.

Harry, picking up his meagre belongings, about to make his way down the moonlit path, stopped in his tracks. Propped against the church wall, near to the steps leading up to the porch, was a bicycle. His initial thought: *What luck!* But was it? It must belong to someone, but who? Did it matter? Why look a gift horse in the mouth?

Glancing furtively around to make sure that he was unobserved, Harry mounted the bicycle. At first wobbling and then gaining balance, he started to pedal. Invigorated, he sped down the lane, bumping over the uneven surfaces. The dim headlight attached to the old bicycle barely picked out the way ahead. Even so with such a clear, moonlit night, it didn't bother him.

His intention now would be to try and pick up the route taken by the cat back to the cottage – the cottage he had found to be Marjorie's home. With this object in mind and not knowing why, he peddled on. It was if he was being drawn back, perhaps, this time to beg forgiveness.

The maze of lanes and countryside may not have presented a problem to a cat, driven by instinct, but to Harry at that hour, uncertain of his sense of direction, it was a daunting prospect.

Now and then dismounting, he assuaged his hunger with an apple or a half-eaten sandwich, kept back for emergencies. But he only stopped for a short while before pressing on, with a view to taking advantage of a full moon lighting his way.

The night dragged on, and with it his weariness. In the copses he heard foxes barking and from the depths of a nearby wood, an owl hooting. Nocturnal creatures, disturbed by his sudden appearance, fled across his path, disappearing into the shadows. Apart from their presence, he felt as if he was the only human at that moment in the world – a solitary figure of no significance.

Some way ahead he spotted a creature going in the same direction. At first, he couldn't make out what it was. It stopped occasionally, lost in the shadows. It then re-emerged, giving a clearer picture. It was then that he realised, to his consternation, that it was the stray dog, the one he had tormented when the whim took him.

The dog, apparently unaware of his presence, plodded aimlessly along. Harry felt uneasy in its company. To his way of thinking, anything could happen on such a lonely stretch of road. So head down, picking up speed, he attempted to pass it. The canine pricked up its ears but otherwise, to Harry's surprise and relief, still ambled along, seemingly uninterested, or so he thought.

Speeding along, his mind dwelling on the accident, his part in it and the long-term effect on Marjorie and her family, he wondered what he would say on his arrival at the cottage. As far as he could see his only course was to face up to and accept the responsibility for his actions. Whilst considering his options and contemplating what might happen, he had become oblivious to his surroundings. Automatically he pedalled on, not caring, until struck by a thought. Where was he? He hadn't the ghost of an idea. But what was that? He could have sworn he'd heard something.

It wasn't the whirr of the wheels, or the miscellaneous noises of insects in nearby thickets. Then what was it? A figment of his imagination? In a pitch-black lane with shadows, was his mind coming into play with all sorts of thoughts and fancies?

Applying the brakes, he stopped, the bike screeching to a halt. A maddening silence prevailed. His senses alert, the hairs standing on the back of his head, he stood at first not daring to look left or right, but the very next second, like a hunted animal seized by fear, he was compelled to by a shaft of moonlight picking out a form – that of the dog.

How it manifested itself in such a way was a mystery, but needless to say, it had. Harry didn't like the way its eyes focused on him, on him alone, its body language giving nothing away.

His knee-jerk reaction was to run, but that would never do. He almost felt that he was dealing with some wild animal, not as he saw it a domestic dog, rather a hostile one.

Keep calm, he thought, *show no fear*. Slowly, he started to wheel the bicycle down the lane, hoping it would tire of its fixation and go away. As he moved away it followed, slowly at first. He quickened his pace, so did the canine. With all his good intentions, Harry, there and then losing his head, mounted his bike and started to pedal for all he was worth, the dog giving chase.

*

In a pool of light lay the boy barely conscious; nearby the buckled remains of a bicycle, a little way away, the dog, badly injured, on its side. Whimpering, it struggled to get up, but weakened, failed to do so.

The doctor on call had been taken by surprise with the events. The main road, although relatively busy during the day, he had found to be free of traffic at night. From a side lane the boy had appeared, riding at speed, followed by the dog, who appeared to be joining in some sort of game that had got completely out of control. The impact, so dramatic with screeching brakes and the smell of burning tyres, shocked the medic to the core. The windscreen crazed, he jumped out.

Harry, consumed with pain, briefly opened his eyes to the see the moon riding silver-rimmed clouds. The face in the moon, the face he'd known as long as he could remember, seemed to be mocking him, as if telling him, "I told you so". Then he heard a sound, that of a dog whimpering mournfully. *Whose dog?* he wondered. He would never know the answer, for closing his eyes, he succumbed.

Chapter 13

'Coming to the pub tonight, Pam?' Robert, his hand on the door knob, raised a questioning eyebrow.

'I don't know,' Pam, stretched out on the sofa, stifled a yawn. 'I feel so tired nowadays, I don't feel like doing anything. It's all I can do to go to work.'

'Come on Pam,' Robert, exasperated by her complacency, frowned. 'Snap out of it, you're beginning to vegetate. Come along with us, it will take you out of yourself.'

'Don't worry, I'll be alright.' Pam, with a soft cushion clutched to her bosom, snuggled down.

Robert shrugged his shoulders. 'Alright, have it your way, but it's no good dwelling on things, what's the use of that.'

A loud blast outside on the horn heralded Ted's arrival and Robert, still not convinced but resigned, leaving Pam to her devices, joined him.

Alone at last, Pam, closing her eyes and laying her head against the cushion, pondered. Why had things gone so terribly wrong? Perhaps she should have gone to the pub with Robert and Ted. As Robert had said, it would have taken her out of herself, even if she wasn't all that keen on watching them play snooker.

In the kitchen, drawing on a pair of rubber gloves, she immersed her hands in soapy water. Get the dishes done and then what? Watch television, read a book or carry on knitting the jumper for Robert, the red one with the reindeers; a complicated pattern, she wished she hadn't started, she hoped it would be ready for Christmas. She stepped over to the window and looked out. At twilight, the witching hour, the kitchen garden appeared tranquil. The vegetable plot where Robert spent hours pottering and the apple tree now shedding its leaves in the dimming light were soon barely visible. The evenings were drawing in and getting colder; with plenty of coal in the outside shed, at least keeping warm wouldn't be a problem. Robert always preferred a coal fire.

On an impulse, making her way into the hall, taking the mouthpiece from the phone cradle, she dialled a number. As ringing, she thought, *I hope she picks up, last time she was in the other room with the door shut.* Just about to replace the receiver, she heard Mary's voice.

'It's Pam, I'm just ringing to see how you are. Robert's gone to the pub with Ted and I'm on my own tonight.'

'It's not good, Pam. There's somethin' wrong wi' Charles.'

'What it it … can I help? Pam, perturbed by Mary's agitated tone, sensed trouble brewing. 'I'll come right over, I'll take the car; for once Robert hasn't got it tonight.'

'Thank you, but no. Ma's stayin' the night, an' I wouldn' want 'e drivin' in the dark. You stay put, don't 'e worry.'

'But what's wrong?'

'It's 'ard to explain, us don't understand it ourselves …' For a moment, Mary seemed lost for words. 'E's makin' an animal sound …'

'He's making a what!' Pam couldn't believe her ears.

'An animal sound, it sounds like a howl, like a dog, or dare I say a wolf, Ma, an' I don't know wot to do. The doctor should be comin' any moment. Charles is quiet now, but doesn't seem to know us.'

'You're sure you're alright, I'd be willing to help.'

'Us'll cope. Thanks Pam, let's 'ope 'tis nothin' to worry about.'

'Bye then, take care.' Pam, replacing the receiver, noticed the free paper on the hall mat. Taking a cursory look through it, and finding nothing of interest, she binned it.

The evening dragging on, she had only herself to blame. She should have gone to the pub. Pam, lighting a cigarette, inhaling and exhaling, relaxed, as watching wisps of smoke curling in the air. Switching on the art deco lamp and pouring out a generous amount of gin with a splash of tonic, she sat down and stretching out her legs, reached for a book.

Sometime later, the sound of tyres against gravel and the slamming of car doors awakened her. The book had fallen on the floor. She bent down to pick it up, rubbing her eyes in the process. She glanced at her watch to find it was 11.30 p.m. She listened to an exchange of voices and the sound of a car's imminent departure, followed by an approach of footsteps and a click as the key turned in the lock.

Robert, his face flushed, bursting with news, pushed open the door. 'I saw the lighted window, so knew you were still up. It's dark out there, you didn't switch on the porch light, I could hardly see the steps. I'm sorry I'm so late. I had a nightcap at Ted's after closing time. I've got something I really must tell you!'

Pam, feeling irritable after such a long evening alone, was not in a receptive mood. 'Can't it wait?' she remarked tersely, 'I feel like some cocoa, would you like some?'

Robert shook his head.

'Well, what is it that's so important?'

'Just before we left, there was talk in the bar of an accident, a fatal one, on the main road not far from the pub. Apparently, the area was cordoned off, some latecomers said. The police weren't answering any questions. On hearing this, those wanting to see, pushing and shoving, made for the door, some the worse for drink. A fight broke out; two men, one with a bloody nose, the other with a cut lip, were restrained by the bartender and another man. Ted and I joined the others, spilling out onto the road.'

'There was no mistaking the spot, some way up the road – it stood out. As we passed, the police were waving people on, we saw an ambulance just leaving, other than that Ted and I couldn't make out anything else, because it was so dark.' He paused. 'You look tired, I should go up now; I'll follow you up in a minute.'

Sleep evaded Pam, she tossed and turned, then eventually giving up, lay on her back staring into the darkness, reliving old memories, happier times when life wasn't so complicated.

Time dragged. She turned on her side to see the bedside clock. Its illuminated hands pointed to a quarter to three. What a long, dreary night! Beside her, Robert grunting, rolling over onto his back, threw an arm across her bosom. A dead weight. Gently prising it off her, she turned over on her other side. Her mouth dry, she longed for a drink of water, but didn't want to wake Robert, instead she tried to get some sleep.

She was just beginning to doze when she heard a noise. Alert, she sat up rubbing her eyes; she switched on the bedside light. It was the doorbell and it was being rung persistently.

'Robert, wake up.' She nudged Robert, repeatedly.

'Go back to sleep, Pam … it's early yet.'

'Someone's at the front door, you'd better see who it is.'

'What, at this time of night! Whatever for?' A disgruntled Robert, heaving himself out of bed, pulled on his dressing gown. 'I suppose, I better,' he groused, stomping down the stairs.

Pam sitting up in bed, clutching the coverlet, listened intently. The voices, were muted and indiscernible, Richard's angry and then subdued.

What was it all about? Had Charles, now in a world of his own, gone berserk? His moods unpredictable, anything could happen. He could have picked up a knife. She shuddered, as envisaging a bloody scene, chaos, the place ransacked. Had James run away? He wasn't a happy boy. Gripped by fear, she imagined an even worse scenario, and where was Harry? Why hadn't he come home or at least spoken to her on the phone?

Then she heard Robert's voice calling her, 'Pam, I think you better come down, there's someone here who wants to speak to you.'

As climbing down the stairs, not knowing what to expect, an awful feeling of foreboding engulfed her. There standing in the doorway was a policeman. On catching sight of her, his face, impassive, gave nothing away.

'Mrs Jenkins … Mrs Pam Jenkins?'

'Yes.'

'I'm so sorry, I …'

Seized by an unthinkable thought, Pam froze. 'The accident, not Harry, it can't be!' Her legs buckling, she swayed – reaching out she clung to Robert's arm, as collapsing, he caught her and held her in his arms.

Chapter 14

A misty rain peppered the cottage window as Mary, opening it, wiped away the condensation. At the sound of the catch, a wet and muddy Tibby, having been mistakenly locked out and mewing plaintively, looked up while padding over the fallen leaves littering the garden path.

Mary, now by the bedside, drawn by the sound of Charles' rhythmic breathing, having slipped a sedative into his nightcap the previous night, studied his face, seeing him seemingly without a care in the world, glad she had.

Haunted by the events of a day she'd rather forget and weary from a lack of sleep, she slipped on her dressing gown and slippers and tiptoed to the door.

Downstairs, she put on the kettle and unlatching the back door, found Tibby on the step. The cat sidling past her, at first prowling as if in search for food, eventually settled down in her basket by the range.

The kettle, boiling for a while, filled the kitchen with steam. Mary, sitting at the work-worn table, chose to ignore it. Then, conscious of a growing humidity, she got up to turn it off, as doing so glancing at the mantel clock. It was quarter to five.

The cottage was as quiet as the grave – restless and ill at ease. Mary, up before the dawn chorus, without any purpose in mind, ascended the stairs. Up in the bedroom, going through the motions, she pulled on her clothes with the intention of going for a walk.

In the kitchen, pulling out and rummaging in the old Welsh dresser for a scrap of paper and a pencil, she scribbled a note to leave on the table.

*

Mary, bemused, wandered aimlessly, the streets empty but for the occasional car – she had come to an impasse, the thick drizzle dulling her senses.

Stonebridge, a maze of streets, shops and alleyways – some areas she had had no need to familiarise herself with in the past. Although unacquainted, she felt at home. No one knew her, no one cared. Yet someone did.

Again, she thought of the doctor's indifference, when without any explanation the previous night, and at some unearthly hour, he had turned up without so much as a by your leave. Some sort of mix-up, maybe. Already low in spirits, she had hoped he might have given a fuller explanation as to the cause of Charles' odd behaviour and some sort of reassurance that any re-occurrence could be modified. Instead, having examined Charles and finding nothing wrong, brusque, his attitude had changed, making her feel guilty for calling him out. Staying no longer than necessary, as an afterthought, he had made out yet another prescription for tranquillisers.

Mary, confused and frightened for some reason by the sound and sudden appearance of a milk float, watched mesmerised as it came nearer, the occupant's face clearly visible. This unexpected encounter disorientated her, throwing her into a panic, and off balance, she tripped on the kerb and fell.

*

'Are you alright?' the voice, at first unreal and then articulate, came close at hand,

She opened her eyes, aware of a presence and then of an image bending over her.

'Here, drink this, it's tea; I always bring a thermos on me round.' He paused. 'What's your name?'

'Me name?' Mary, glancing up at the milkman's friendly, yet worried face, struggled to think. 'Can't remember.' Gripped by a sudden spasm of fear, she stared at him. 'Me name? Don't know it, do 'e?' her voice, pleading, seemed far away.

Perplexed, the man shook his head. Putting a reassuring arm around her shoulders, he said, 'My dear, you're not at all well. You shouldn't be wandering around the streets in this weather. Here ...' He indicated the milk float, parked by the kerb, 'You come with me.'

Although at first uncertain, Mary willingly obeyed and with his help struggling to her feet, blindly followed him.

The milkman, driving a short distance down a side street, stopping the float outside a corner shop, smiled, and patting her on the arm, said, 'You stay here, I won't be a moment.'

After a while, through the lighted shop window, she saw the milkman and presumably the shopkeeper engaged in what seemed to be a lengthy conversation. A woman joined them, and the three of them, still talking, came out of the shop and stood on the pavement, looking in her direction. Consequently, at first, Mary experienced an overwhelming desire to run away, but instead submissively sat there trying to ignore them, but to no avail.

The woman, breaking away from the others, approached the float. 'My name's, Ethel,' she told her, on drawing abreast. 'Come into the warmth, my dear,' she said, pointing to a shop still ablaze with lights in the grey dawn light. 'You'll catch your death of cold out here.'

Mary, following her, found herself in a cosy backroom where Ethel had taken control of the situation. Dry and wearing borrowed clothes, she sat by an electric fire with a mug of hot, sweet tea, which soon revived her. Although at first distressed because of her lack of identity, now she didn't care but rather enjoyed it. Reassured, the milkman resumed his round, leaving her behind. There she would stay, not knowing the distress her condition had caused, both at home and in the strange surroundings she now found herself in.

Enquiries were being made. With the police having been informed, "missing persons" notices were pinned up at strategic places in the town.

At first, on finding Mary's note, Amelia had assumed that

although a break from routine without any clear explanation was not Mary's style, she would, however, be back in no time. But would she? With doubts and dark thoughts crowding her mind, she telephoned Malcolm, thinking for some reason she had gone to see him. But finding this was not the case, she telephoned the police station, who having taken her daughter's description, put out a call. A call eventually leading to her whereabouts.

*

Amelia and Malcolm, on finding the corner shop, and having been ushered into the little back room by the shopkeeper's wife, had found a stranger. A different Mary, not the warm-hearted and loving person they'd known but one that barely looked at them.

'I expect you will want to speak to her … that's if she recognises you.' The woman mustered up a smile. 'If there's anything you want, just give me a call.' Making for the door, she closed it behind her.

Mary impassive, Amelia and Malcolm, pulling up chairs, sat down beside her.

'Mary, it's Ma, don't 'e know me?' Amelia, reaching out, caught hold her hand.

Who were these people? She wished they would leave her alone. Mary, her thoughts muddled, a wooden expression on her face, snatched it away.

Amelia, shocked and hurt to the core by her reaction, tried again. Pointing to Malcolm, now standing by her chair, she cried, 'This is Malcolm, surely 'e remembers 'im … and Marj, yer daughter in hospital!'

Mary, unmoved, just sat. Her face was the face of a stranger, one who clearly wanted to be alone.

In desperation Amelia, as white as a sheet, glancing at Mary and then Malcolm, exclaimed, ''Er doesn't know us … Wot's goin' to become of Charles?'

Chapter 15

Jeremiah, having closed the vicarage gate, looked up at the sky, a grey sky, with spits and spots of rain. On opening up a newly acquired golf umbrella and dodging puddles from a previous downpour, he was dismayed to find his cassock splattered in mud.

At the end of the lane, shrouded in mist, loomed the farmhouse and outbuildings. Behind them, surrounded by a stark outline of trees, the church, bleak in the gloom, seemingly epitomised the forthcoming event.

Of Harry Jenkins, he had little recollection. The Jenkins family had hardly ever attended the church services and Harry had always appeared elusive and antisocial.

The lychgate creaked, as pushing it and passing through he attracted the attention of a lone figure, crouching by a grave. The man, attired in a heavy navy-blue serge coat, on his head some sort of peaked cap, was wearing a stout pair of boots. Who was he? The vicar had never laid eyes on him. A seaman or a fisherman? In the dim light, he couldn't tell. But he intended to find out.

'A relation or perhaps someone you knew?' Jeremiah asked, on drawing abreast.

'I thought so, but it ain't. I must 'ave got me lines crossed.' The man spoke in the deep phlegmy voice of a heavy smoker – a man of the open air, more than likely, he smelt of the sea.

Intrigued, but lost for words, Jeremiah then said, 'Well, I must press on, a funeral you know.' On second thoughts, adding, 'But we really must have a talk when I'm free, then maybe I can be of help. Come inside for the service, do.' An invitation rejected out of hand, prompting him to add, 'Perhaps not, but if you did, at least you'd be in out of the rain.'

On leaving the stranger, and on approaching the church

porch, a feeling of curiosity compelled him to look back. The man, now standing up, appeared to be studying him, caught unawares. Doffing his cap, he bowed low, revealing a mop of unruly red hair.

*

The church, its interior reverberating to the sound of organ music, was packed to its capacity. A subdued congregation, punctuated only by an occasional bout of coughing, whispered conversations or signs of recognition acknowledged with a nod or smile, was soon to be overshadowed by the ominous clang of the church bell.

At that moment, all eyes turned towards the heavy oaken door as it opened to admit the bearers. Six men shouldering a pine coffin – gracing the top, a centrepiece of yellow, bronze and rust chrysanthemums in a circle of white. Pam, supported by Robert and Oliver, followed behind. Bereft, in mourning, attired in a black, two-piece costume and cream blouse, her blonde hair tucked under a large picture hat of the same hue, a veil concealing a tear-stained face, sombre-eyed, she looked straight ahead. Ted and his wife were followed by various family members and close friends, some nodding as passing down the aisle, others deep in thought.

With the coffin coming to rest before the altar steps, Jeremiah, up in the pulpit, clearing his throat, looked down at a sea of expectant faces. After a false start with a baby crying and an errant child, severely disciplined and left to sulk in silence, he started the service.

At the request of the family, he had just begun a brief synopsis of Harry's short life, and was endeavouring to paint a rosy picture, when, jarring, the church door swung open. In the doorway, with his back to the light, stood his former churchyard acquaintance. Cap in hand, looking somewhat embarrassed, not knowing what to do, he looked this way and that. Jeremiah indicated a pew at the back, much to the annoyance of its occupants, who already short of space, were obliged to move closer together.

The vicar, slightly annoyed when picking up the threads of his sermon, was even more so with the man's lackadaisical attitude on such a sad occasion – rough looking, he just didn't seem to care. A stranger, who was he anyway?

In the front pew, Pat, gripping her prayer book, glanced at her husband. His brother, Patrick, true to form, had caused a disturbance at a time of deep sorrow. Although on the surface, whatever they were thinking, both Robert and Oliver had shown little emotion. Her blood boiled. The insensitivity of the man, turning up like this out of the blue and on such an occasion! *What did he want and why?* she wondered.

When moved by the evocative strains of "Yesterday" and "The Fool On the Hill", those of a previously unknown pop group, who having shot to fame overnight, were now currently in the charts, she stopped caring. The lyrics, lovingly played by Oliver at the organ before an enraptured gathering, brought back memories. "Yesterday", Harry, her youngest, a constant worry. Should she have supported him, advised him, not given up so easily? Would it have changed things? "Day after day, alone on a hill, the man with the foolish grin is keeping perfectly still, but nobody wants to know him. "The Fool On the Hill", played with such feeling, emotionally charged, she questioned herself, Could that have been Harry? With a lace edged handkerchief, she wiped away a runaway tear.

*

'Stop fidgeting, James!'

'It's me collar, it ain't right, do I 'ave to wear it?' James twisted around in his seat. 'Who's that man them people are lookin' at. I ain't seen 'im afore.'

Ruby, exasperated by James' behaviour, raised a finger to her lips. 'Be quiet, people are looking at us.'

'Why me, yer talkin' as well, ain't you?'

Wagging her finger, she retorted, 'Aren't you, not ain't you

– diction, James, diction, sit up straight, stop slouching.'

James, shrugging his shoulders, muttered, 'I wish Harry was alive. Us 'ad such fun and 'e loved the Beatles, 'er wouldn't understand.'

*

The mist was clearing and although damp underfoot, there had been no need for umbrellas at the graveside. The small group that had gathered to witness the interment had dispersed, leaving Amelia alone. She had left Charles with Malcolm by the lych gate and was just thinking of rejoining them, when she heard a familiar voice.

'Mary, where's Mary?'

Amelia, on turning her head, was surprised to see Pam. ''E gave me a fright.' Wot's 'e doing there?'

Pam, wiping her face with a tissue, remarked, 'What a sight I must look.'

'No, 'e's alright; us thought 'e looked smart, you're bound to be upset.'

'But where's Mary?'

'Us didn't 'ave time to tell 'e, that is, 'bout what's happened – her's lost 'er memory.'

'Her's lost her what! You did say memory?'

Amelia nodded.

'How did it happen?'

'Dunno, the doc says 'er may or may not recover. 'Er been worried 'bout Charles, wondering where 'it was all going to end. 'Er still don't know us. 'Er's 'ome with us now. 'Er's with the neighbour. 'Er's been so good, although us never 'ad much to do with 'er.'

'How's Charles taking it?'

''E's changed. 'E wouldn't know him. 'E's been tryin' to help us; we hope it lasts. Still one can only hope and pray. I'd better go; they'll be looking out fer me.' Amelia smiled – laying her hand on her shoulder, she said, 'The darkest night comes

69

afore the dawn, 'e'll find time heals.'

Yes, perhaps you're right, Pam thought, as watching her walk away. A thought soon overshadowed by another. Why had Patrick attended Harry's funeral and in such a way? Who had told him of Harry's death? She would never know, for Patrick had simply vanished.

*

Malcolm glanced at his watch, and then down the lane for signs of the taxi.

'Wot's that, I thought I heard somethin'? There it goes again, it sounds like a cat.' Charles, propelling his wheelchair towards the boundary wall to steal a look, exclaimed, ''Tis Tibby, wot's 'e doing here, old girl?' Charles reached out to touch her. Tibby, crouched on the wall, still doubtful of Charles' intentions, instinctively withdrew.

''Er ain't so friendly with me,' commented Charles, ''ow's that?'

'Where's Amelia? The taxi will be here soon,' Malcolm, otherwise engaged, frowned. 'Ah, there she is.' He gave a sigh of relief.

''Bout time too,' said Charles, raising an eyebrow. 'Where 'ave 'e been?'

'Talking to Pam, tryin' to help her.' Turning her attention to Tibby, who having met her had followed her back, she mumbled, ''Tis an omen.'

'Wot?'

'Tibby, how did 'er find 'er way here? Is 'er tryin' to tell us somethin'? I 'ope Mary's alright.'

Chapter 16

'Time will heal,' Amelia's words at the graveside still fresh in her mind, Pam, walking slowly up the garden path, paused to reflect. And time had, but very slowly. At first an almost unbearable pain, an emotional one, which she as a mother must accept and live with. But as the days wore on, with the subsequent passage of time, memories dimmed. It was a gradual wearing-down process, or so it seemed to her. Her only fear, an ever decreasing clarity of Harry, the person for what he was. His freckled face, unruly red hair and green eyes, eyes that signalled his every mood, now no more. How could she forget his pouting lips, his daring – her youngest son, who liked to live life to the full? A rebel without a cause, just like his Uncle Patrick.

It was the so-called insignificant things she missed at first. Harry had always been so untidy, she'd found herself forever picking up after him. She was forever tripping over discarded trainers, cups, saucers or plates, left on the carpet where Harry had sprawled, watching television in a constant state of disarray with a devil-may-care attitude, which irritated, urging her to comment, 'I'm not your servant.' But now freed from her bondage, it was just a memory. Tears brimmed with a stark reminder. No longer the mischievous grin with a shrug of the shoulders in response to her frustrated pleas, but instead without him, everything in its place where it should be. Her heart ached for what had been. Seeking relief, she worked longer hours, coming home late, tired and still despondent, when needs be to an empty house.

Robert whiled away his evenings in the pub; for he too had had difficulty in coming to terms with Harry's death and like Pam blamed himself for the way things had turned out. Needless to say they hardly saw each other, and when they did, inevitably quarrelled over matters of little importance.

Pam, making a superhuman effort to turn out Harry's bedroom one afternoon, to sort out and dispose of articles of clothing and personal effects, on pulling open a number of drawers, found them crammed with all sorts of oddments. Wondering how to dispose of so much junk, for she had found little of value, she was just thinking of piling it back, with a view to binning it, when a scrap of paper caught her eye. On picking it up, she found in Harry's untidy scrawl, a name and telephone number – the name illegible.

Downstairs in the hallway, acting on an impulse, reaching for the telephone, she picked up the handset and dialled the number, the very next moment losing her nerve, quickly replacing the receiver. She pondered. A thought occurred, *In for a penny, in for a pound*, the words boosting her confidence, she dialled again.

''Ello …' a woman's voice responded. ''Ello, 'ello, if yar takin' the mickey, I'll git the Garda, that I will.' She spoke with an Irish accent.

'I'm Pam Jenkins, I've reason to believe my son Harry's been ringing this number.'

''Arry who? Oh 'im, 'e's always ringin' 'ere to speak to Patrick. 'E's 'is father, I suppose.'

Pam, beginning to weary of the woman's attitude, retorted, 'No, his uncle, that's if it's any of your business. Shall we get to the point, please.'

''E needn't speak to me like that, I'm only tryin' to help.' She paused. ''E owes me six month's back rent and now they tells me 'e's dead. I'm not made of money. Who's going to pay me; that's what I want to know?'

'Dead! But he can't be … how, when?' As if in a dream, it occurred to her as she spoke that she would never see Patrick again, and Robert, already on a low ebb, how would he react to the news? That's if the woman was telling the truth.

''E's dead alright,' the woman's voice cut across Pam's train of thought.

''E was fighting over some painted trollop, worse for drink

an' all, an' not fer the first time. This time 'e fell overboard and drowned, so they tells me.' Silent for a moment, she then asked, 'You ain't one of 'is fancy women?'

'Certainly not!' Pam raised her voice. 'I'm his sister-in-law.'

'Don't 'e get all uppity with me!'

Pam glanced at her watch. She'd had enough of a conversation she was finding increasingly distasteful, so commented abruptly, 'I have to go, anyway, thanks for the information.'

'Begorra! ...'ow 'bout my back rent, who's goin' ...'

Pam slammed down the receiver. So Patrick was dead. She didn't know whether to feel sorry or glad. The bottom of the barrow, he was a rotten apple and like Harry had come to a sticky end. It was only to be expected. And as to that woman, goodness knows what Harry had been up to when her back was turned.

After a while, pulling herself together, she made her way into the lounge and glanced out the window. It was getting dark, the street lights casting ominous shadows over hedgerows and pavements, not a soul to be seen, only the occasional cat on the prowl, on the chance of catching a mouse. Etched against a sombre sky, a flight of birds winging their way home to their nests. The silence only broken by the click of the garden gate. Peering out she saw Robert. Worse for drink, he was staggering up the garden path, at times falling down in the process. Giving him a cursory look, she sighed, as drawing over the curtains. *What was the use of breaking the news to Robert,* she thought as climbing the stairs, *Wasn't he acting just like Patrick?*

Upstairs in her negligee ready for bed, Pam knew what she was in for – a sleepless night, with a consistent pounding on the front door, slurred speech, and persistent requests, 'Pam, le' me in!' In an effort to ignore him, turning over on her side, she reached out and switched on the radio, at that moment not caring if he slept outside on the step all night.

The thumping with expletives seemed to go on forever, and then a blessed release, and with it silence. Her nerves stretched to breaking point, Pam switched off the wireless and pulling the coverlet up to her chin, lay staring into the darkness. For sometime she listened out, her senses acutely aware of any movement or any noise, but the silence prevailed, and with it memories came flooding back.

Fleeting snapshots of schooldays, of Robert standing by the gates, waiting to walk her home, offering to carry her satchel or books, a lock of dark hair falling over his forehead, as with a mischievous grin, he pushed it aside. Their wedding day, the joy and pain of giving birth, watching Oliver and Harry, in turn, grow and mature. On reflection, their marriage had started to go downhill at this stage, as gradually drifting apart. Most of the time she was fully occupied bringing up the boys – less mindful of Robert, leaving him lonely, resentful, out on a limb. At first, the thought of Robert going to the pub with Patrick to play an occasional game of snooker or darts had seemed a good idea, and she saw no harm in it but was pleased for him, not knowing how things would eventually turn out.

She fell into a fitful doze, waking spasmodically. On hearing the sound of a distant car's engine, she drowsily conjectured as to where the driver was journeying and why at that time of night. The droning sound of a plane comforted her, the occa-sional hoot of an owl a sign she was not totally alone.

A persistent summons of the alarm having invaded her senses, sleepily stretching out to turn it off, Pam knocked it clattering onto the floor. She sat up in bed and having swung her legs over the side, stooped to pick it up. The grey light of dawn was stealing below the curtain line, the silence broken by a marauding cat at issue with an adversary. She pulled back the drapes to see, but saw nothing, the cat having slunk away, with or without its prize. And so should she. Refreshed even from a small amount of sleep, Pam there and then came to a decision. She dressed, washed and tidied herself, then pulling a heavy suitcase down from the top of the wardrobe, preceded to fold and pack clothes, underwear and toiletries, as having completed her task, lugging the case to the door.

Downstairs, she picked her way around Robert, fanned

by soft breezes, he was lying face downwards, the front door having been left wide open. With a last disdainful look at him, Pam, picking up her handbag and manhandling her suitcase, stepping out onto the path, shut the door behind her.

Chapter 17

'I'll be down the garden.'

Amelia, standing at the sink, although not turning around, aware of Charles' presence, asked, 'Do 'e need any help?'

'If 'e could just push open the back door.'

Amelia, wiping her hands on a tea towel, obliged, having done so, leaving Charles to his own devices.

The garden had long since reverted to its wild state, weeds predominant in the fight to take over, almost obscuring the garden path with a stranglehold. Charles' futile attempts to remedy the situation by pulling up an occasional weed, barely making any inroads.

Amelia, watching him through the kitchen window, although relieved at his change of attitude, felt sad and abandoned at the same time.

Mary, well wrapped up now, sat under the old, gnarled tree at the bottom of the garden most afternoons, Charles habitually joining her. Together they'd sit for an hour or two in companionable silence, watching the world go by – that is, wildlife and habitat – in the back garden. Whether she recognized him, Amelia had no idea, for nowadays Mary, registering no emotion, stared vacantly ahead.

With the advent of autumn, the air keener and the nights colder for a short period, a feeling of quietness and tranquillity was experienced by all in the little market town. Plumes of smoke spiralling into a grey, sombre sky, from myriad cottage chimneys, acrid autumnal smells of crackling bonfires, flames leaping, sparks flying.

Malcolm having made her a cat-flap, Tibby, with the approach of winter, sought refuge in front of the range when the whim took her. Although still cautious of Charles' intentions, every now and then she would sit by his side. Malcolm, between visits to the hospital, came and went, sometimes sleeping overnight in Marjorie's old room. Always attempting to put on a brave face, an inspiration, he had given Amelia the strength to carry on.

The break-up of Robert and Pam's marriage had been no surprise to Amelia. In these troubled times, it seemed to her that anything was possible.

Pam, for the time, had gone to stay with her mother and as far as she was aware, with Robert at home – Oliver, who had gained a degree in agriculture, there with him. With Oliver willing to help out, and Christmas in the offing, Ted had made an allowance for Robert's unfortunate relapse.

One afternoon, just as Amelia was about to feed the hens, there was a knock at the door.

'If 'e let's me out, I can feed 'em once I lays me hands on some cornmeal in the shed.' Charles nudged the backdoor.

Amelia having opened it for him, on answering the summons, raised an enquiring eyebrow when finding Ruby and James standing on the doorstep.

'We've called in on our way from the hospital. Ma wanted you to have some home-made jam and a meat pie she'd made, which she thought you'd like and asked us to pass it in on our way home.'

Amelia, taking the proffered plastic bag, exclaimed, 'How thoughtful of 'er.' She mustered up a smile. 'It must have bin a lot fer 'e to carry, with all them other things as well.'

'No, it's no problem; James has to take his turn, haven't you?' Ruby cast a hawk-like eye.

James, tight lipped, ignoring her, his eyes fixed on the ground, at that moment presumably focusing on a snail's slimy progress.

'Speak when you're spoken to,' she cried, 'else I shan't take you to the pound tomorrow after school.'

''E's going to the pound, 'ows that?' Amelia frowned. You ain't goin' to get a dog, is 'e?'

'Us is,' James suddenly came to life. ''Cos I wants one.'

'We *are* – diction, James, diction!' Ruby, having tapped her brother on the shoulder, said, 'You see Ma thinks it will be company for him, but says he's got to look after it, else it goes straight back to the pound.'

'I promise I will,' James' eyes widened, 'cos I want a friend, I'll call 'im …'

Amelia feeling a modicum of pity as ruffling his hair, said, 'I suppose 'e misses Harry.'

'Yes, cos he was me mate.' James looked and felt down in the mouth.

'How did 'e find Marjorie?' Amelia asked, glancing at Ruby.

'Just the same, Malcolm was there, he was looking tired.'

Amelia, aware that the light was fading, commented, 'You'd best get going afore darkness sets in. It was good of 'e to visit Marj, and call in with the jam an' pie. Don't 'e forget to thank yer Ma fer me fer …'

James, butting in, cried, 'I needs it don't I? 'Er don't understand, it ain' the same without Harry anymore!' Looking defiantly at Ruby, he exclaimed, 'Anyway, what's it got to do with you … you gets on me nerves, 'e's always bossing me 'round.'

'That's enough of that!' Ruby retorted. 'Keep your opinions to yourself, else I'll tell Ma.'

'Tell-tit, tell-tit!'

Ruby stared at James, who avoiding her gaze, subsided into silence.

'But I needs a friend, don' I?' James appealed to Amelia's good nature.

''E will if yer Ma agrees.' Amelia patting him on the shoulder, smiled. 'If 'e's meant to have one, 'e will.'

'Mrs Tucker doesn't want to know about our problems,' Ruby spoke in a sharp tone of voice. 'We called in to see if we could help out in any way, you know, shopping, anything that needs doing.'

Quite touched by their concern, Amelia said, 'Run along 'ome, else I shall be worried.' She smiled as watching them making their way up the garden path – Ruby, berating James in her customary manner, with him as usual losing the battle.

Amelia, with darkness descending, on her way down the

garden path, someway ahead, could see Charles obstinately fumbling with the latch of the hen house. He was determined to help in any way he could, and although puzzled at times because of this change of attitude, she could not help but admire him. Gone was the old Charles, the one that sat in the corner and sulked. He looked up as she approached, his face creasing into a smile, he cried, 'I'll get the 'ang of it if it kills me.'

Amelia laughed. 'Us wouldn't want that,' she said, 'would us, Charles?'

'Three eggs. What do 'e think?' he asked, holding them up for her appraisal.

'Us has 'ad more, but I'm not grumbling. Them's better than none.'

'Us'll have 'em fer our breakfast.'

The lone figure sitting silently under the branches of the old tree attracted Amelia's attention.

'How be feelin' today, Mary? Us'll be having eggs fer breaky, won't that be nice?'

The blue eyes, set in the pallid face, gazed at her vacantly.

Amelia shivered. A thought occurred, *It's getting chilly, an' the sky clouding over, soon a pitch black, I blame meself, I shouldn't let 'er stay down 'ere so long.*

With so many things to do, there weren't enough hours in the day and time flew, hence the neglect. She must make up for lost time.

''Tis too cold fer Mary, I be taking 'er indoors. Don' 'e stay out too long, else 'e'll catch yer death of cold.'

'Don't 'e worry, I shan't be long. Just a few minutes longer.'

Amelia, having taken Mary's hand, led her up to the cottage. In sight of the back door, she was taken by surprise as the cat flap sprung open. Tibby with a mew and tail erect, came padding down the path to meet them.

Mary, who up until now had not registered any emotion, started to speak. Listening intently, Amelia was just able to make out the word, 'Marj's.'

In response, Tibby, rubbing his head against Mary's legs,

purred as if in acknowledgement.

Charles, by the henhouse, with its occupants locked up for the night, mused. He gazed up at a sky, coal black, pinpointed with stars, and at the brilliance of a crescent moon, near to which a bright star indicated a fine tomorrow.

Chapter 18

What a mess, Oliver thought, *How am I going to cope?*

The place was a tip; Robert had lost all sense of reality. In an alcoholic haze, he lolled around the cottage, apparently not knowing nor caring. His increasing lack of interest in food coupled with a growing obsession for the bottle concerned Oliver. He didn't go out and spent most of his time asleep when not drinking, then waking up with a hangover and reaching for another, for the "hair of the dog".

In desperation, Oliver had made an appointment to see a doctor on his behalf for help and advice. This turned out to be a thankless task, when subject to abuse, with Robert in self denial, he had been made to feel guilty.

In the lounge, before leaving for work, Oliver drew back the curtain and looked out the window. A thick, misty drizzle and a dove-grey sky indicated a miserable aspect. The grey Austin van, faithful to the last, parked by the old stone wall, covered in globules of water, his passage to work. He had taken the keys and hidden them, for although it was Robert's van, he had no intention of letting him loose in it. Initially, there had been a row about this issue, but like everything else, Robert had lost interest.

Quite frequently, on his way home, he called at his grandma's house to see his mother. There he generally had a meal and this was now becoming a regular occurrence. Pam had washed her hands of Robert and refused to discuss the matter. She was now forming new friendships and interests, consequently turning her back on the old way of life. Torn between the two, Oliver felt sad and frustrated. Ted, Robert's business partner, also concerned, had drawn him aside in his office to discuss the issue. When airing his views, he left Oliver even more perplexed by highlighting a problem only he could solve.

*

Robert, opening his eyes, at first in his befuddled state didn't know where he was. Slouched on the settee in his everyday clothes, his head ached. His mouth dry, with shaking hands, he reached out for a non-existent bottle and finding none, cursed. His breathing shallow, in an attempt to get up he lost control, only to fall back again with the effort. On his feet at last, he swayed, then staggering to the door flung it open with a view to getting some fresh air. The daylight bright, he shielded his eyes from a glare so different to the dim interior.

Outside in the garden, the cool air having revived him, a need for a drink drove him on. Like a man on a mission, looking under bushes for containers of any description, in any likely place he may have forgotten when hiding yet another bottle. He longed again for the warm glow of amber liquid, which temporarily blotted out his insecurities. "Mother's Milk", he recalled. Hungry too, Robert couldn't remember when he had last eaten, that's if that mattered when he had a bottle in his hand.

Back in the lounge, he picked up a framed photograph of Pam and himself on their wedding day. To him, it seemed as if he was looking at another person, a person so far removed and yet so familiar. Acutely aware of his self-inflicted exile, embittered and angry without the drink, he just had to give vent somehow to his pent-up emotions. So acting on the spur of the moment, he picked up the photo frame – anger induced, he threw it, threw it with all his might across the room.

As if in a dream he watched it, as if in slow motion – it hit the wall, shards of glass peeling off in every direction. The release of tension experienced through this act of wanton vandalism giving him a sense of purpose, his eyes now focused on his next potential target – Pam's art deco lamp. Confused and upset, with its imminent destruction he thought of the way she had destroyed him. Thinking of her, he picked it up and threw it as forcefully as he would have her, watching its demise as it shattered with a sense of satisfaction.

Once he'd started he couldn't stop. Hell bent, he embarked on a trail of wanton destruction. In a haze, oblivious to the damage he was inflicting on his surroundings, he hit out again and again. By the time he'd finished it looked like a bomb had hit the room. Overturned chairs, with the dining table upended, Oliver's electric guitar wrenched from its socket, smashed against the wall. In a blind rage, in the heat of the moment, sheets of music discarded as confetti strewn across the room in an act of revenge, against a son who cared. His blood-shot eyes seeing a prized French carriage clock, lying in the grate, he had felt no remorse. A family heirloom, irreplaceable, of no significance to him. Over the fireplace, an oil painting, recently purchased in an art gallery as an investment, its glass crazed; a tapestry over the lounge door hanging at a crazy angle, everywhere chaos! Barely recognisable, the carpet, a pale-blue Axminster, now a muddy grey, littered with broken china and anything that had come to hand when out of control, he had vented his wrath.

Worn out at last, Robert, hollow-eyed, having righted it, slumped into a chair. In the prevailing silence, staring vacantly into space until ultimately subdued, he then rose to his feet.

In the kitchen, whilst still hunting for a bottle, which might miraculously manifest itself, he assuaged his hunger with a left-over chicken carcass. In the waste bin, on finding a bottle, he was delighted and then disappointed on finding it emptied, presumably by Oliver. Tipping it up, he savoured the last drops.

The afternoon wore on and with it, Robert's despondency. On occasions he fell asleep, only to be awakened by some imagined horror, shaking and perspiring in a now darkened room, cold and alone.

The grate in the lounge, as usual, had been stacked neatly with sticks of firewood and old newspapers by Oliver, ready to light on his return that evening. Near to the fender, a box of matches caught Robert's eye, and drawn to the spot, he picked them up. Still in need of a drink, his body shook. He stared at the matches, at the floor strewn with the chaotic mess he had created all around him, to him a visual symbol of what he had become.

He closed his eyes, hoping things would go away – on opening them, finding them still there. Drawn to the matches, he emptied the box. He struck a match. It flared; mesmerised, he watched it as it temporarily lit up the dim interior. Crouching on the floor, he struck another, then another – then on an impulse, as spotting the wedding photograph now without its frame, set it alight. The flames taking hold, the edges turning brown, the images distorting, the photo twisting and curling as if in agony, he thought of what might have been, and wept.

Chapter 19

Malcolm pulled up the collar of his coat as passing through the gates of the garden centre. It was raining, a fine drizzle, not to be underestimated, penetrating even the thickest of coats. Head bent, he made for the bus stop, cursing his lack of foresight.

All day the sky had made no secret of its intentions, with a grey, menacing aspect, and clouds scurrying across its wide expanse, driven by a wind gaining in strength.

He generally relied on his alarm clock to wake him, but to his annoyance, that morning, it had let him down. Had he over-wound it or simply forgot to set it? He didn't stop to find out. Throwing on some clothes, grabbing some toast, a hastily made mug of tea, one last look around to see he hadn't forgotten something, and he was off.

It was not a good way to start the day, and he had become increasingly irritable as the day wore on, knowing well the weather was deteriorating and that he was ill-equipped without a mackintosh and umbrella. It was especially annoying as he was intending to pay a visit to Marjorie at the hospital after work. Thank goodness he had had the presence of mind to bring some money for a cup of tea and a plate of sausages and mash in the new work's canteen at lunchtime. Still hungry and un-sustained, he felt miserable.

The centre's stock of fireworks for Guy Fawkes' Night soon depleted, on November 5th, on one of his numerous visits, Malcolm was to find Tibby cowering under the kitchen sink, a place where Amelia had found it difficult to retrieve or placate her. That evening, by Amelia's side, he had stood in the doorway with Charles and Mary, watching a colourful but noisy display of fireworks, with rockets soaring to the heavens. In a pungent atmosphere, listening to the cries of children grouped around a nearby bonfire, with memories of a year ago not far away, the local fire brigade, now giving a sigh of relief, had just been called out to a minor incident.

*

The Oasis Garden Centre with Christmas goods on display was now a hive of activity with people coming and going, as Malcolm had known it would be. Tinsel and snowmen, and not one, but several Father Christmases, having become an everyday occurrence – not forgetting the reindeer, especially Rudolf – to him, all of which, although not religious, so premature, spoiling the true meaning of Christmas. The strings of coloured lights, pretty and cheerful throughout the long winter days, he thought, not a good idea, with customers lost in a frenzy of spending and preparation. *Call me Scrooge, I don't care,* he thought, with customers coming and going.

At the bus stop were many fellow employees, intent on a night out. 'There's a good film at the Regal,' said a lanky youth with pimples. 'A horror film, how about that?' He ogled the girls, his suggestion going down like a burst balloon.

'I'd rather see Cliff Richard again in *Summer Holiday*,' chipped in Mitzi, an office worker, dreamy eyed when thinking of Cliff.

'Snooker at the pub?' said a crew-cut lad, stubbing out a cigarette with his winkle picker.

'I can't play snooker and I don't drink,' said Jenny from the plant department, eyeing the youth, 'better you didn't.'

'I wouldna like to spend Christmas with you!' he rejoined, to laughter.

Another employee, a mini-skirted, red-haired girl surrounded by admirers, suggested dancing.

'Catch me dancing?' cried a dark-haired youth. 'I wouldn't know 'ow to anyway.'

'Well, it's about time you learnt,' Sandy retorted, 'can't you even rock 'n' roll?'

'What do I want to do that for?' he asked, his colour rising.

'Because everyone's doing it, aren't they? Really, don't you know anything?'

'What if they are? I aint!' he smirked, flicking back his hair with a comb. 'I'd rather play a Beatles' single.'

The other youths laughing, rather self-consciously, somewhat relieved when seeing the long-awaited bus.

Malcolm along with the others, boarding it, not wanting to be involved, sat near the front. With the bus pulling away, the chatter and fits of laughter of those in the back grew louder.

Malcolm, having rubbed away the condensation, peering out at an ever darkening countryside, pondered: how many more times would he make this journey? Would Marjorie ever recognise him, or forever remain in a coma?

After a while, the bus slowed down in response to a siren. A fire engine suddenly appearing out of the darkness provoked an interlude of profound silence and speculation.

Malcolm, who up until then had been deep in his own thoughts, looked out of the window just in time to see the vehicle vanish with blue lights flashing. *A fire, or a road accident, or rescuing an injured animal, which one?* he wondered. Whatever it was he wouldn't be on time at the hospital.

The bus moving at snail's pace, they had not gone far when it came to a halt, flagged down by a policeman, who spoke to the driver.

'I'm afraid you can't come this way, sir, there's been a fire and the area's closed off.' He smiled, and pointing to a fork in the road some way ahead, went on to say, 'There's a diversion. It's clearly marked. Sorry for the inconvenience.' This having been said, standing aside, he waved them on.

Malcolm, looking out the window, had seen and heard enough to get the gist of the conversation. His heart sank. He glanced at his watch as he thought he would be late. Conscious and responding to pangs of hunger, now a constant reminder, he planned ahead. Was there a chip shop or café near to the hospital? He would hope so.

At the back of the bus, Sandy, the girl in the miniskirt, was not particularly pleased with the unexpected hold up, as the boys, now bored, had become unruly and were teasing her. Tiring of their company, she could be heard telling them in a loud voice where to go and what to do.

A wind picking up, the driver, having taken the advised route, had made little progress when hampered and restricted behind an ever increasing tailback of vehicles. The occupants in the bus subdued, in the front, Malcolm losing all sense of time. Try as he might, he couldn't recognise any familiar landmark. At times, looming up out of the gloom, spotting a signpost in the glare of the bus's headlights, he tried but failed to read the place name.

Passengers were getting off. With hardly anyone else on the bus, apart from a few others, he was to find himself practically alone. At last, a series of street lights enabled him to discern familiar landmarks – after a long, drawn-out journey, he was nearing his destination.

On approaching the hospital, a familiar figure hurrying in front of him caught his eye. It was Amelia. In an effort to catch her up, he increased his pace. As if aware, she turned, and catching sight of him, exclaimed, 'Malcolm, what a surprise. What's 'e doing 'ere at this hour?'

'The bus diverted, with a backlog of traffic due to a fire it's taken an age to get here. Anyway, I'm here at last, and glad to see you.' A smile played around his lips.

'Was 'e coming to see Marj?'

Malcolm nodded.

Amelia, catching hold of his arm, gave a sympathetic smile. ''E looks all in. Come home with me after us have seen Marj an' have a bite to eat.'

Climbing the steps to the main entrance, Malcolm, almost at the top, stopped to listen.

'What's wrong?' Amelia, clutching his arm, raised an enquiring eyebrow.

'I thought I heard something, but must have been mistaken … It's been a long day. Come on, let's go in,' said Malcolm, pushing open the swing door, 'It's cold out here.'

Chapter 20

The cottage on the outskirts of Stonebridge stood in an idyllic setting, access gained by crossing a little humpbacked bridge spanning a stream. To its rear, pastureland stretching as far as the eye could see, to a backdrop of distant woodland.

In the little room, with a persistent summons of the bedside alarm shattering the silence, Pam awoke with a jolt. *Time for work already? Oh no, hang on a minute, what day is it?* Propping herself up on one elbow, on reaching out to switch off the clamour, a bright thought occurred. Of course, why hadn't it occurred to her before? It was her day off, and Joy was coming to pick her up.

Pam, wiping the sleep out of her eyes, slipped out of bed. Glancing around the semi-darkened room, she yawned. The wallpaper, the chintz curtains, even the smell, everything just the same. The attic, filled with childhood memories, captured her imagination, even though she had never thought of herself as sentimental.

Once her world, nothing had changed. The same nursery pictures easily identified in the half light, the little dressing table by the window, her old teddy, now much the worse for wear, still in its place on the chest of drawers in the corner. Together, she and Dad in the distant past had named him Roosevelt. How the years had flown. Dad having passed away after a painful illness, leaving Miriam, her mother, to soldier on alone.

Pam, drawing back the curtains and opening the casement window, found a quieter morning than of late, with no wind and a hint of the sun. Near the windowsill, the old apple-blossom tree, now stripped of its foliage, standing stark and bare, its gnarled trunk, down which she and her brother had shinned all those years ago, still sturdy and strong.

The staircase creaked as Miriam, with a tray, lifted the latch.

A gentle breeze brushing the net curtain, on seeing Pam by the open window, she commented, 'I should close the window, before you catch your death.'

Pam, eyeing a mug of tea and a plate of digestives, said, 'There was no need for that, I was just getting dressed.'

Miriam shaking her head, not taking "no" for an answer, put them down on the makeshift bedside cabinet.

'Oh Ma, you do fuss.' Pam squeezed her hand. 'I'm not your baby anymore.'

'But you will always be to me. I just want you to be happy.' Miriam fluffed up the pillows.

'Don't worry, I'll be alright given time,' Pam cried, climbing back into bed.

*

'I enjoyed that.' Pam, seated at the kitchen table, placing her knife and fork on her plate, pushed it aside. 'I've wiped the platter clean.' She dabbed her mouth with a serviette. 'Bacon and eggs, you spoil me.'

'It will set you up for the day.' Miriam, having cleared the table, carried the dishes to the sink.

'By the way, I've been meaning to tell you …' Pam took a sip of tea. 'I bumped into Amelia the other day. She told me in passing that James is going to have a dog. What do you think of that?'

'I don't know what to think.' Solemn-eyed, Miriam, noncommittal, shrugged her shoulders. 'But you can understand why; he's lonely without our Harry, they went everywhere together.' She mustered up a smile. 'I suppose it will work out. Let's hope so, for his sake. I'm glad he's joined the Boy Scouts, that way he'll make friends. Anyway, what are you doing today?'

'I'm meeting Joy.'

'Joy?'

Pam, in reaction to Ma's enquiring look, told her: 'You know, the woman I told you about, the one I met at the dance on Saturday. She's a young divorcee, but apart from that, good company.'

That's all very well, but be careful.' Miriam frowned. 'I don't want you to get in with the wrong crowd, especially now.'

Pam, laughing, cried, 'What, me at my age? There's not much chance of that. I've a grown-up son and I thought I had a husband.' She pursed her lips. 'Anyway, since I haven't, that's enough of that. Joy will be here any moment and I mustn't hold her up. She'll want to dash, she's thinking of exchanging her old banger for a new Morris Mini-Minor, they're all the rage now.'

'Where does the money come from?' Miriam's eyes widened. 'She must be made of money.'

'She's the manageress of one of those new boutiques; they're springing up all over the place.'

*

Alone at last, Miriam, sitting at the kitchen table, thought how times had changed. Who would have thought there would be so many woman driving cars of their own? No good would come of it in her opinion. The world had gone mad. Dad, bless his soul, would have had a fit. The way she was talking, it seemed that Pam would be having a car herself before long – she hoped not. To be sure, no good would come from her friendship with this woman, Joy. But Pam had made up her mind. The Green Shield Saver Book left lying on the table, with thoughts of Christmas, turning the pages, she switched her mind to the number of stamps required.

At the sink, having piled the dirty dishes into the washing-up bowl and leaving them to soak, she decided to take advantage of the sun.

Should she sit in the garden, or having caught sight of some swans in the stream through the window, feed them with crumbs? A question posed and unanswered when the phone rang.

It was Oliver. 'It's Dad,' he said, trying to hide the tremor in his voice.

*

Pam, waiting outside on the grassy verge, cogitated. Miriam worried about her, but then she worried about everything. Worry got you nowhere. Life a gamble, one had to take risks, didn't one? One way or another, it was up to her to make the most of her life. *Snap out of it,* she told herself, with the Austin A40 rounding the corner, and Joy's cheery face behind the wheel.

Joy, bubbling with enthusiasm, pulled up and beckoned her to climb in. 'I'm glad you're on time,' she said. 'I promised I would be in the showroom on the dot. My, what a dream!' Her eyes misted over as taking in the cottage. 'And an 'umpback bridge an' all! I'd love to live in a place like that.' She sighed, 'Still, with my lifestyle it would never work – I'm always out. Give it a slam,' she said, indicating the passenger door. 'You know what it is; I've been meaning to have it fixed at the garage.'

On their way, now and then with Joy's eyes fixed on the road ahead, Pam glanced at her profile. Joy was attractive, she had to admit, high cheekbones, thick, dark hair and flawless skin. Still she was a good deal younger than her. The way she dressed too, with a figure to match, offset with the latest fashion – an observation doing nothing to boost Pam's already flagging moral when thinking of her wardrobe.

She let Joy prattle on, as silently thinking her own thoughts. With a better job, she could look just as smart as Joy. 'I've worn well for my age,' she muttered, 'haven't I?'

'Did you say something?' Joy's voice jerked her back to the present.

'No, just talking to myself.'

'First signs, they say, don't they?' Joy grinned. 'Anyway, you haven't heard a word I've said … about the fire.'

'What fire, where?' asked Pam, her curiosity aroused.

'I'm not sure. Anyway, we haven't got time to discuss it now, I'd better put my foot down, else we'll be late.' Joy, gesturing dismissively, drove on with a will.

Chapter 21

'Come on, sis, you'm holding us up, us'll miss the bus,' shouted James, as racing along the pavement towards a queue of people lined up at the bus stop.

'There's no need to shout, I'm not deaf,' Ruby gasped, as panting and puffing, with James, she joined the queue just in time to catch the bus.

'I told 'e, us might 'ave missed it, I ain't always wrong,' James said, as along with others they climbed aboard.

*

Ruby had never visited a pound before and wondered what to expect. Seated behind the driver, James, who was usually subdued in her company, was chattering incessantly, his face flushed with excitement.

The conductor, with a smile, attracted by James' enthusiasm, asked, 'Is it his birthday, today?'

'No, we are just going to the pound, that's all,' Ruby said, in bored tone of voice.

'Oh, I see.' The man, picking up on her lack of enthusiasm, without commenting further, passed down the aisle.

Ruby, trying to ignore James' inane chatter, feeling tense, with the chance of an oncoming headache, closed her eyes. *I hope Ma realises what James is taking on,* she thought.

On their arrival and after passing through the iron gates, their attention was drawn to a run on their right, in which a number of dogs of miscellaneous breeds and ages were romping around, barking excitably, Ruby wriggling her nose when taking in a strong smell of disinfectant.

James, entranced by a spectacle of so many dogs, riveted to the spot, to her relief, for once, saying nothing.

Lying close to the netting, nose on paws, was a rather large brindle-coloured dog, who, unlike his companions, showed no desire to play. His eyes fixed on the gate, never moving as if waiting and watching for someone or something. James, absorbed with the antics of others, had passed him over, but not so Ruby. Intrigued by the dog's vigilance she approached, and kneeling down, in a kindly gesture, stretched out her hand. Her heart went out to it as, detached and seemingly sad, the dog seemed unmoved by her friendly overtures. It was as if the canine, as almost losing heart, had all but given up with its lonely vigil.

'I see you're interested in Charlie,' a voice said.

Ruby looked up to see a fair-haired kennel maid carrying a bunch of keys.

'I'm Tammy, I was just coming to clean out the run when I saw you with him.'

'Is that his real name?'

'No, we don't know it, but we like to give each dog a handle, that is if they haven't got one already. Are you really interested in Charlie? Most people don't give him a second look.'

'Why?' Ruby, feeling increasingly sorry for Charlie, wondered what had gone wrong. Had he been cruelly treated?

'Perhaps because he looks so miserable; he's not what you would call "full of fun". I suppose it's his history.'

'His history?' Ruby, intrigued by the dog's despondency, wanted to know more.

'Can't tell you much. All I know, he was brought in by a man who didn't leave his name and address. No one seems to know anything about it now, but I intend to find out. The trouble is, there's so little time. We've so many here to keep track with, it's all we can do to feed what we've got on a daily basis. Come to think of it, there was another dog but it ran away, so I've been told. But other than that, I haven't a clue. It's sad, I suppose, in a way.' Her brow puckering, she stopped to think. 'I should be getting on with my cleaning, but if you're really interested, I'll …' She glanced at the dog, his eyes still fixed on the gates. 'Dear of him, he deserves a break.'

'It's my brother who wants a dog. That's him over there.' Ruby pointed to James. Someway off, he was still watching the other dogs. 'I'll have to see what he thinks.'

Later that day, in the bus homeward-bound, James, silent and subdued, sitting beside Ruby, looked out the window.

Peering sideways at his profile, Ruby commented, 'Are you alright, you're very quiet?'

In response, James having suddenly found his voice, rejoined, 'What do 'e think? I ain't got no dog, 'ave I, 'e promised, 'e's let us down.'

'Don't be silly,' she said, thinking, *How like James, to want something right away.* 'Grow up!' she snapped. 'You can't pick any dog; you need to pick one that suits you. Do you understand?'

James nodded. A glum expression on his face, he sank back in his seat.

Ruby, feeling a modicum of pity, then said, 'Trust me, I know what I'm talking about. If you'll be content to wait for a dog, and it's the right one, then it will be content to wait for you.'

*

James, Dog at his heels, having picked his way over the tumbled masonry, passed the burnt-out shell that once was Harry's home. A large, rough-coated dog, brindle coloured, with intelligent eyes partly obscured by tufts of hair, no longer sad, but alive with a knowing expression, was watching its master's every movement.

Alone, Ruby had been making her way home from the hospital, and having called on Amelia was nearly there, when she first saw the dog. On her approach, it had greeted her like a long-lost friend, nudging her persuasively, its tail wagging, whimpering, pleading for affection. It was the dog from the pound.

'I'd better take you back,' she'd said.

Collarless, the dog had willingly run through the streets beside her. *Ma will wonder where I've got to,* she thought. But it has to be done.

Once again, inside the gates, the canine had tentatively lifted a forepaw and looked up at her. In that short space of time, a bond had been forged between them, as far as it was concerned. The dog, baffled by her tone, had stood its ground. When, steeling herself, she had said, 'This is your home, you don't belong to me,' she had not looked back, although having handed it to a kennel maid, she had been aware of it watching her departure.

As the weeks passed, James, although initially keen on having a dog, had been unable to make up his mind. His negative attitude had irritated Ruby; she was beginning to think she was wasting her time, and this just another way he had of manipulating her.

On a rainy evening on her way home from the hospital, Ruby had been fumbling in her handbag for the key to the front door. Amelia had been pleased to see her, but with the weather closing in, she hadn't stayed long. Home again, Ruby, her head bent against the driving rain, having found her key when making up the garden path, had become aware of a presence. The dog, sitting on the doorstep, its fur wet and muddy, had shook itself, spraying her with rainwater. It had looked so woeful, that on such a wild night she wouldn't have wanted to turn it away.

'You'd better come in,' she'd said. 'I won't be taking you back this evening.'

Chapter 22

Amelia now read to Mary each afternoon for an hour or two. On other occasions, they sat and listened to the radio – Amelia hoping to get some sort of response, some indication of recognition, perhaps a breakthrough. With the onset of winter, each day was drawn out and dreary. Tibby joined them, if anything a welcomed addition, her presence was soothing and unhurried as she sprawled by the fender in the warm confines of the kitchen.

Now and then Amelia could have sworn she had a fleeting glimpse of some sort of expression, or awareness, on Mary's face, but tended to dismiss it as wishful thinking.

She had not seen James since he had acquired the dog, but had heard a lot about it. It seemed that things were working out, better than she would have thought. Charles too, who would always be wheelchair bound, had come to terms with his disability and like Malcolm was willing to help in any way he could. Frequently seen resolutely propelling the wheelchair along the pavements, at first suspect, Charles now had acquired a circle of friends, some old and some new. He too had seen James with the dog at a distance, but not to speak to.

Charles, sitting in front of the range with Amelia and Mary one stormy afternoon, remarked, 'It's so snug and warm in here, I don't really want to go out.'

'There's no need,' Amelia said. For a while they'd lapsed into silence, each with their own thoughts, the only audible sounds the ticking of the kitchen clock and Mary gently breathing as she slept. The silence was at last broken by Amelia, who said, 'For a while, 'er's at peace.'

*

She had never known how it had happened and almost given up trying to bring it about, when a combination of events produced the desired effect. That unforgettable day when Jeremiah had called, they had been sitting in the parlour, discussing forthcoming church activities, when she'd heard a scratching noise. Was it Tibby wanting to be let in? If so she would have to wait. Why hadn't she used her cat flap? Amelia, annoyed, chose to ignore it. But the scratching persisted, leaving her no alternative but to apologise to her guest to go and investigate.

She had left Mary asleep in her usual place by the range, and on entering the kitchen had been taken back to find her sitting up, fully alert, holding in her hand a sharp knife. Alarmed at the sight, and expecting the worst, she was about to take it away when she realised what she had been doing. Mary, having picked up a tin tray lying near the fender, fully absorbed, had been scratching away on it. Overwhelmed with curiosity, and seemingly unobserved, she approached, and leaning over her shoulder, tried to see why. At first, Amelia could not make any sense of the meaningless scrawl, but on closer observation, had been able to decipher the words, "Tell Marj I love 'er."

Elated at first by the thought of a possible breakthrough, she was to find it short-lived, Mary quickly reverting. Her momentarily absorbed and alive look back to what it was before, wane, distant and vacant. It was as if it never happened; had she really imagined it? But no, crystal clear, there was the evidence in front of her in the form of a crude scrawl on the tin tray. With the passing of time, and Malcolm calling around, but not so frequently, Amelia, busy, put the experience behind her.

Chapter 23

Slamming shut the door of the old A40, Pam, rolling down the window, said. 'We shan't be long.'

Amelia, standing at the gate, waved until the vehicle vanished out of sight. With the weather on the turn, the sky a steely light-grey, there had been warnings of snow. A nip in the air, she shivered as anticipating the signs and hurried indoors.

'I'd best go down bottom fer some more coal.' Charles, dozing by the range, awoke with a start on hearing Amelia's voice. She stooped and, picking up the coalscuttle, said, 'Let's hope us don't 'ave the falls us 'ad last year. Them blizzards an' them heaps of snow.'

In the process of stoking the fire and clearing the ashes, Charles did not answer her at first, the fire spitting and sending up sparks, Tibby protesting, making for the cat flap. Then over his shoulder, he said, 'Who can tell what's 'round the corner, best us don't know.'

*

'Isn't it about time you took your coffee break, Malcolm, I think there's a lull.'

'Thanks, that I will, that's if you'll cover for me.' Malcolm smiled at Maureen. A tall, shapely girl, she was always trying to mother him. He watched her. Unaware of his scrutiny, intent on rearranging the items on her gift counter to their best effect, she was leaning over, a curtain of light-brown hair falling down around her shoulders. He watched her with mixed emotions. If he hadn't met Marjorie, perhaps … As soon as the idea occurred to him he dismissed it, knowing well it was not wise to indulge in such flights of fancy.

Finding a corner table, he relaxed with a coffee. His mind a blank, revitalized by the strong, hot liquid, he lazily observed the comings and goings. The restaurant filling up, he had been lucky to find a place just in time. His feet ached, even so he had reluctantly agreed to work extra hours with the build-up to Christmas. Aware of the increasing hubbub, stretching out his legs, he closed his eyes in an attempt to switch off. Unable to relax, he was just figuring out how and when he would be visiting the hospital again, when he heard a familiar voice. On opening his eyes, for a moment unable to locate the speaker, he spotted her.

Pam was sitting with Mary at a table near to the entrance. Frustrated, without any success, she had been attempting to engage Mary in conversation. Her eyes lighting up on catching sight of Malcolm, she beckoned him over.

'It's looking quite festive; it's surprising what can be done,' she said, taking in the atmosphere, 'with tinsel, holly berries and Christmas lights. There might have been a bigger tree, although why should I care, I'm not in a Christmassy mood this year.'

'I'm not surprised, what with Harry and now Robert ...'

'Thank you for your sympathy,' she said, butting in. 'That's all water under the bridge. Life goes on, as you well know.'

Malcolm, momentarily at a loss for words, wondered what to say next. Wasn't he too at a crossroads? In an attempt to change the subject, he asked, 'What's Oliver going to do, now?'

'If you mean, where's he going to live? – he will be living with Ma and me of course,' she sighed. 'There's nowhere else for him to go. He'll probably move into a flat in due course.'

A pause in the conversation, Malcolm, the silence bearing down upon him, found words tripping off his tongue: 'He could share mine, until he finds somewhere else.' What had possessed him to say that, he wondered?

Pam, with a flicker of a smile, replied, 'Why, that's so nice of you, I'll tell him ... Anyway, why not have a spot of lunch with us here? I'll pay.'

Touched by her generosity, Malcolm said, 'I was going to the pub for a pre-Christmas drink. A few of us get together from

the department in the lunch hour, for drinks and a bar snack …
but under the circumstances, I don't think they'd mind. If you're
sure, I'd love to join you.' Glancing at his watch and getting up,
he said, 'I'll have to get back, I'll see you later on.'

'How's it been?' Malcolm asked Maureen, on his return.

'Quite quiet, except for the odd body who told me it's started
snowing. It always looks so pretty, but I hope we don't have any
problems like we had last year.'

At lunchtime, on his way back to the restaurant, Malcolm
encountered Pam.

'Where's Mary?' he asked.

'I've left her inside in the warm,' she told him. 'I've been
out looking at the snow and I'm quite worried. My car's an old
banger and I haven't really got used to the controls.'

'You could phone for a taxi, and while you're waiting have
something to eat, a bowl of soup or something.' He frowned. 'On
second thoughts, the taxi may have problems getting through –
at the look of the sky we may be in for a blizzard.'

*

'Are you warm enough, Mary?' Pam, having wiped away the
condensation with an old rag, set the window wipers in motion.
'Here, take this blanket and wrap it around you.'

Mary with a haunted look, snatching it from her, snuggled
down in the passenger seat.

Affectionately known as the "Old Bus", at first protesting,
with Pam behind the wheel, the car finally lurched forward,
then, roaring into life, took to the road.

At first the snow had lined the tarmac with just a thin layer,
but trodden in with the passage of vehicles, it was becoming
treacherous. Here and there a broken down vehicle, abandoned,
skid marks telling their own story. Pam, driving cautiously,
now and then stole a sidelong glance at Mary, who, seemingly
unperturbed, was gazing out the window. Satisfied, Pam turned
on the headlights, their beam picking up the ridges of solid ice

forming on the road's surfaces. There seemed to be no let up with a blanket of snow over wayside verges, hedges and distant trees, transforming a once familiar landscape into a winter wonderland.

Tempers flared as an ever increasing tailback of vehicles inched forward. Some drivers arguing with others, their voices clearly heard on the still icy air.

Pam, becoming aware of a Mini nudging her rear bumper, glanced in the rear-view mirror. A new Mini? She took a second look only to discover that it was a Morris Minor, driven by a man or woman. At first, she couldn't tell which, the driver's vision currently obscured by condensation. The driver, as it turned out a woman, with the aid of a rag and window wipers soon remedied the problem. She could have sworn it was Joy.

Mary by now asleep, Pam, in a never-ending line of traffic, applied the handbrake, as coming yet again to a halt. Bored and wondering whether it was Joy, she took another look in the mirror, the Morris' headlights temporarily dazzling her. It was then, without warning, the car started to roll forward. In a daze, having thought she'd applied the brake, her foot, down hard on the pedal, ineffective, she tried the handbrake, but the car continued to slide on the road's slippery surface towards the car in front.

Helpless, it seemed to her as if the car had a mind of its own, as out of control, gathering momentum, it lurched forward. She grasped the steering wheel; wracking her brain she tried to remember – one always steered into a skid, didn't one? Whatever, it didn't work, and she found herself rapidly approaching the verge, the wheels spinning. On the point of impact, violently thrown forward, she clasped her hands over her head without thinking. Her back and neck feeling sore, a wetness tricking down her face, for a while afraid to move, she sat as if in a dream. Conscious of an urgent rapping on the driver's window, she was about to wind it down, when a voice beside her said, 'Where am I?' Mary, it was Mary … My God, she'd forgotten all about her. With great misgivings, she took a cursory look to find Mary, having swivelled around in her seat, sitting up eyeing her with a questioning look.

Miraculously, she seemed relatively unharmed, although missing was the withdrawn look, as if in the agony of the impact a barrier had come down revealing the old Mary, the one they had loved and known so well.

'Did 'e hear me, Pam? What am I doing' in yer car? What's happened, 'e's bleeding? Oh, my God! Who's lookin' after Charles?' Her voice tinged with fear, she wrestled with the door handle. 'Let me out!'

Taken aback with this unexpected turn of events and completely lost for words, Pam was no match for her barrage of questions. Once again aware of a persistent rapping on the window, she wound it down, mechanically, to see a man's concerned expression.

'Are you alright?' he asked.

For a moment, Pam just looked at him, then in a subdued voice, said, 'I ... think so.'

'She's not; that's obvious,' chipped in Mary.

'I saw it all,' said the stranger. 'Very nasty. She's in shock.' Then turning to Pam, who had still not responded: 'Keep still in one position; you may be injured.' Then next, when addressing Mary, 'Are you alright?'

'I'm fine,' she replied, 'though lord only knows 'ow I got 'ere.'

Slightly confused, the man said, 'Maybe you're in shock too, but keep an eye on her,' he said, indicating Pam, 'while I go and get help.'

*

Malcolm, after a long day in the gift shop, on returning to the flat exhausted, had gone to bed early. At first lying awake, then falling into a fitful sleep, he'd dreamt he was chasing someone across a beach. His feet, barefoot and bleeding, he could feel the sand between his toes, the pebbles and outcrops of rocks impeding his progress, the girl always someway ahead of him. The roar of the surf like thunder in his ears, with seagulls circling overhead seemingly mocking him, weakening his resolve, tiring, his movements becoming slow and sluggish, as on and on, he ran. Then rounding a rocky outcrop, he saw her standing at the water's edge. On his approach, turning, she smiled and beckoned. It was Maureen.

He awoke with a start. The dream still fresh in his mind, with an overwhelming sense of shame, he didn't attempt, as dressing, to analyse its meaning. In the bathroom, glancing at himself in the mirror, a thought occurred, *Did women find him attractive, or did he just arouse their maternal instinct?* A train of thought soon broken with a knock on the door.

'You're wanted on the phone. Are you alright? The colour's gone out of your cheeks.' His landlady, standing outside in the landing, appraised him.

'Quite alright, thank you. Someone on the phone?' *Now who could that be?* he wondered, knowing well that Mrs Piper never asked their name.

By the hallstand, on lifting the receiver, he was surprised to hear Oliver's voice.

'I thought I'd let you know that Ma and Mary have been admitted to hospital for observation. Ma's car skidded on ice. Don't worry, they're alright. There's nothing to worry about. By the way, I'd like to take you up on your offer. If it still stands, when can I move in?'

Chapter 24

James, trudging through the snow with Dog on his weekly visit to the hospital, found himself enjoying the experience. The heavy snowfall overnight had disrupted the traffic; the gritters were out. In the company of others, James was making his way on foot.

He had no hang-ups over the chaos, to him it was a novelty. Should there be another fall of snow, with luck, school would be cancelled. There would be snowball fights to look forward to with his newly acquired friends, many of whom belonged to the Cubs or Scouts. He'd built a snowman in the garden and with Christmas just around the corner, who could tell what might happen. Much to James' amusement, Dog, at first mystified by the snowflakes, had raced around in circles barking excitably, but now by his side, had settled down.

Ruby, his sister, had left school and was now working in the local supermarket, a relatively new acquisition and way of shopping in the town – a place she thought, as others, to gain work experience, while waiting for her A-level results. Now not having to look after James, relieved of the responsibility, it pleased her to see him partly through the dog's companionship, making friends of his own. Her brother, gaining in confidence, not so argumentative, was beginning to stand on his own feet. James having exhausted his grief for Harry, it appeared, had moved on. But as for Dog, from the moment she had first clapped eyes on him in the pound, there had been something about him, something familiar, but what? Meanwhile James, knowing that Ruby had strongly advised him against taking Dog to the hospital, had given in to the canine's persistence.

Unbeknown to James, some way behind him, the fair-haired girl picking her way in the same direction had recognised the dog. Her heart warmed to think "Charlie" had at last found a friend, having been at one time so concerned for the sad-looking mongrel that nobody wanted, the one with a history. Pulling up her collar as looking up at the sky, she hurried along, with the anticipated snowflakes starting to fall. Ahead of her the boy and dog disappearing from view, she thought no more about them, having other things on her mind.

*

'You stay 'ere, 'till I comes back, do 'e 'ere me?'

At the sound of James' voice, Dog wagged his tail, at the same time eyeing him with a trusting but somewhat questioning look.

James, having searched his pockets, and finding an old piece of rope, attaching it to Dog's collar, secured it around the nearest post. Seeing no harm in leaving him near to the hospital entrance, he then mounted the steps without a backward glance.

*

Left alone in the driving snow and still unaccustomed to the white powdery substance, Dog, at first subdued and then affected by the noise, hustle and bustle, became frightened. Not understanding, cautious, his animal instincts preparing him, had he been left again? Picturing another time, restrained behind netting, then watching the gate, he whimpered, then pawing the ground he strained at his bondage.

'What are you doing here, Charlie?'

With the fair-haired girl approaching him, Dog in response to the familiar voice pricked up his ears in an attempt to greet her. Barking, he broke free. Disoriented by his strange surroundings and new-found freedom, he panicked at first and then picking up James' scent, scampered up the steps into the hospital.

*

Amelia stopping in her tracks, as pushing Charles down the long hospital corridor, stepped aside just in time as the spectacle streaked by. The dog, a large, rough-coated one, dark brown, was very wet and barking frantically. It stopped momentarily to shake itself vigorously, and then with the passage echoing with the sound of voices, raced on. The very next moment, a nurse accompanied by an orderly, and a fair-haired girl obviously in pursuit, having materialised, promptly vanished.

'Well, I never!' Amelia exclaimed, looking at Mary. 'Nothin' will surprise me now at my time of life, but in a 'ospital of all places.'

Dismissive, but as usual sticking to the point, Mary commented, 'There's nothin' us can do, is there Charles?'

'Suppose not,' he replied somewhat reluctantly, adding, 'but 'e could cause an awful accident, 'specially in a place like this. An' wot 'bout hygiene?'

''Ere, let me take a turn.' Mary, making a move toward the wheelchair, was immediately held in check by Amelia.

''E'll do no such thing,' she cried, ''e'll soon be back in 'arness, don't 'e worry 'bout that.'

*

James hadn't relished the idea of visiting the hospital on his own. He saw no point in a lonely vigil by the bedside, finding it boring and time consuming, his eyes inevitably drawn to the wall clock, as if by a magnet, counting the minutes. If it hadn't been for the bribes, the extra pocket money Ruby had forked out from a frugal pay packet, saying, 'Do it for me James; she's my friend, it will mean so much,' he would have refused point blank. Still what had he to lose, especially with nowhere particular to go and no one at home? Should there be no school due to the weather, he'd probably make a few detours on his way back and by chance meet up with a few of his mates in the back lane, behind the old cinema, to smoke a few fags. With this in mind, he fingered the damp cigarette packet lodged in his pocket, and pulling it out, found he had only two Woodbines left, the tobacco having spilled out, making a soggy mess in the pocket lining. Looking at the offending items, he shrugged. He didn't really like smoking, it made him feel sick but he had to, hadn't he, else he wouldn't fit in and may be ridiculed. He couldn't risk that.

He sighed and picking up a discarded magazine lying on a table near to the window, flicking through the pages without much interest, he glanced at the clock. Maybe if it had been a *Beano* or *Dandy* it would have been easier to bear, for he followed the exploits of Desperate Dan with interest. By the window, he looked out to find it was still snowing, the sky a sullen grey. While drawing his woolly jerkin around him, he heard a noise – it came from the direction of the door. Semi-ajar, swinging open, through the gap he saw a whiskery nose. The door opened to reveal Dog. James keeping a firm grip on his collar, Dog in turn, rope trailing, pleased with his exertions, tried to nuzzle his face, his tail wagging, with short, sharp barks conveying, "I've found you, aren't I a clever dog?" His master's nerves were at breaking point in such quiet surroundings.

Closing the door, having released his grip, James, sitting on a chair by the window, wondered what to do next. Dog, making a beeline for him, resting his head on James' knee, gazed up into his face. For a while he sat, stroking and scratching Dog's ribs, while the dog, in ecstasy, closed his eyes. Then realising the gravity of the situation, he admonished him. With flattened ears in reaction to the verbal onslaught that followed, 'Bad, bad dog!' Dog, dejected, sprawling in front of James, nose on paws, eyed him with a sad and mournful expression.

'It ain't no good looking at me like that.'

Dog, lifting his head, snuffling in recognition, took this as a signal to lurch forward, this giving a chance to sit close to James' feet.

''E can't stay here.' James, screwing up his face, frowned. 'I shall 'ave to hide 'e, but where?' For a while he pondered, then lowering his voice to almost a whisper: 'I knows, under the bed, and don't 'e move,' he said, raising his voice to emphasise the point. 'Do 'e hear me?'

It proved an arduous task, for anxious as Dog was to please his master, the dark, cramped space didn't appeal, as crouching on all fours, he awaited events. Bored with the game, Dog made several attempts to emerge, only to be unceremoniously shoved back. Worn out with his exertions and the worry of it all, James, wiping the perspiration from his brow, sat down, unthinkingly, with a bump again on the chair by the window.

It had stopped snowing and a weak sun was attempting to make an appearance, its rays filtering into the room, casting its glow on the figure lying in the bed. The only sound breaking the ensuing silence, apart from an occasional snuffle from under the bed, was the relentless ticking of the wall clock. James hoped and prayed that Dog would not let him down. He had no plan as yet; if only an emergency exit or a side door used by the staff would avail itself. He had no recollection of seeing any. There again, he hadn't been looking out for any. Perhaps he should take a chance and leave the room with Dog in tow, hopefully without anyone noticing – any thoughts on that score dashed on hearing voices and approaching footsteps in the corridor. Nervously, he glanced in the direction of the bed, acutely aware of the dark shape crouching beneath it eyeing him contemptuously, the door opening with the footsteps slowing their pace.

In the doorway, having pushed it open, stood Mary, clutching a bunch of flowers. 'Wot's 'e doing 'ere then?' she cried, on catching sight of him. 'Ain't that kind of 'e, to come?'

James, uncertain what to do, at the same time surprised at this chance meeting, for a moment, was dumbstruck. Finding his voice, at last, he managed to stammer, 'I ... I thought 'e'd lost yer memory.'

Touched by his reticent manner, Mary, managing a smile, said, 'I might of, but I've found it.'

Feeling rather out of his depth in a conversation he wanted no part of, James, prevaricating, said, 'I best be goin' now.'

'Can't 'e stay? 'Ere 'ave a sweet.' She brought out a paper bag. ''E'll like 'em. Won't be long 'til the others are 'ere.'

'No thanks, I best be goin' home.' James, suddenly remembering Dog, the next moment appearing to change his mind, then said, 'But it ain't teatime yet, so I could hang around 'ere, a little longer fer Marj.'

''E's become a good boy, haven't 'e, since …?' Mary, smiling her sweetest smile, didn't mention Harry.

James, colouring under her gaze, exclaimed, 'Do 'e think so?'

'There 'e is; I've been wondering 'bout 'e. Have 'e seen the dog?' Mary cried. With the sound of footsteps in the hallway, and Amelia at that moment entering the room pushing Charles in the wheelchair, the conversation had come to an abrupt end.

'Can't say I 'ave.' Amelia, bringing the chair to a standstill and having applied the brake, sitting down on the nearest chair, wiped her brow.

Were they talking about Dog? James, curious and yet alarmed at the thought, ventured, 'Dog, what dog?'

'Us couldn't catch it. It were like a streak of lightning rushin' past,' Charles frowned on recall.

'Yes, 'elpless, us could only stand back an' watch it go.' Amelia pursed her lips. 'It ain't right letting animals loose in hospitals.'

'Wos anyone chasin' it?' James asked, as feeling uneasy with Dog under the bed.

'A nurse, one of them orderlies an' a fair-haired girl.' Charles up until now had been studying James' reaction. 'Why, 'e don't know anything 'bout it, do 'e?'

'No, I don' know anything, 'onest. I would tell 'e,' James' response, so immediate and on the defensive, convincing Charles otherwise. Wisely he didn't pursue the subject, without proof, he wouldn't have wanted to make a fuss.

As they spoke, they heard a number of footsteps echoing along the corridor, a door slamming and then silence. Again the footsteps, this time louder, the door swinging open revealing a nurse asking, 'Have you seen a dog?'

Each of them shaking their heads, except Amelia, who

wanted to know what it was like.

'Large, scruffy and wet,' she said, with an air of distain. 'The sooner it's caught, the better.'

Standing immediately behind her was a male orderly with a fair-haired girl who informed them, 'The dog's name is Charlie, it was a rescue, but recently adopted; I recognised him. I'm a kennel-maid at the pound.' Then turning to James, she said, 'Your face is familiar, now where have I seen you before?'

'I've done nothin'.' James, avoiding her gaze, toyed with the zip on his jerkin. 'I best be going, else Ma will be wonderin' where I be.'

Undeterred, the girl said, 'But surely …' At first puzzled and then struck by a thought, she exclaimed, 'Now I remember: you were with a dog, I saw you some way ahead of me on my way here in the snow. It was Charlie … where is he now?'

''E's … 'e's …' James, flustered, with a burning desire to escape, with or without Dog, rambled on, 'I'd best be goin' home, Ma …' all the time edging closer to the door, stopped in his tracks by the orderly, who in an attempt to grab him sent a chair clattering to the floor.

Under the bed, Dog, still sulking about his unexplained exile, pricked up his ears. James' tone and body language had upset him, what had he done wrong? Feeling threatened and confused, his senses unwittingly reliving old memories with emotions running riot, when remembering the netting, watching the gates and now again in the cramped darkness, not understanding why – would there be another door slammed in his face? Dog, whining and stretching out his forepaws, inching his way forward, thrust his whiskery nose out from under the bed.

'What's that?' asked the nurse. 'I thought I heard something; why it's the dog. Quick now, help me catch it before it gets away again.'

Ensconced in his vantage point under the bed, Dog eyed the group suspiciously, as attempting to encircle him they slowly approached the bed, but they were no match for him. Still wet and dripping water, Dog, seeing his chance, took it, and finding no means of escape when confined to the room, rushed around, jumping on and off the bed, humping his back, his tail tucked between his legs, barking noisily. This for a while held his audience spellbound, until tiring with his activities, coming to rest in a corner, he slumped down, panting.

For a while, the figure in the bed had lain unobserved and forgotten, but now all eyes focused on her, shocked and dismayed by the dog's apparent loss of control and of any injuries she may have sustained.

The nurse, bending over, looking up and smiling at the circle of anxious faces, said with gusto, 'No, not a scratch, it's a miracle, no more or less.' Her voice hardened, 'Now let's deal with that dog.'

James watched her with mixed feelings, as turning her attention to Dog still crouched in the corner. *What now?* he thought.

Quite annoyed, but very tentatively, she made moves towards Dog, who, cornered, looked wildly about, his eyes eventually alighting on James.

'Call him to you, can't you? It's your dog,' the nurse cried, gesturing impatiently.

'Yes … I,' James, stammering, stood riveted to the spot.

'Well, what are you waiting for?' she said sharply, fixing him with a glare.

Aware of her hostility, James was just about to do what she wanted when a moan, barely audible, was heard coming from the direction of the bed. In no time, grouped around, each individual, some doubting the credibility of what they were witnessing, would see Marjorie's eyelids flickering, her eyes slowly opening.

For a moment, Marjorie lay there, a bewildered expression on her face.

'Marj, it's Ma. Can you hear me?' Mary bent over her. As if afraid of breaking the spell, she spoke in a soothing tone, choking with emotion on seeing a smile of recognition.

'How nice to see you,' Marjorie cried. 'Wot am I doin' in bed? An' who are all these people?'

Mary, overcome, sobbed; her tears falling unchecked, she clasped Marjorie to her breast, gasping, 'Marj … thank God, 'e's back in the land of the livin'.'

No one noticed James and Dog taking their leave, James closing the door silently behind them.

Chapter 25

Tim's leave had come as a surprise. Since having not been long back in camp, he had not expected to be home for Christmas. Standing for a while on the station platform, beside him his kitbag, in it hastily bought presents, tiring of the wait, slumping down on the nearest seat, he placed his head in his hands.

'Goin' home fer Christmas, son?' On raising his head and looking in the direction of the voice, he perceived an elderly man, sitting on a nearby seat, smoking a pipe. 'Yer a bit late ain't yer?' he said, 'T'will be Christmas Day soon, won't it?'

'Yes, but I'm on my way now; better late than never, don't you think?' Tim, feeling tired, not wanting to engage in a lengthy conversation, got up. Slinging the heavy kit bag over his shoulder, and wishing the old timer, 'Merry Christmas,' he mustered up a smile. In response the man, with a toothless grin, doffed his flat cap.

Tim, having made his way to the edge of the platform, along with others waiting for the train to appear, looked down the railway line. The air frosty, its banks steeped with snow around and about, a milling crowd with an air of expectancy had eyes fixed and ears trained on the darkened tunnel.

'Have you seen the station master, I've been looking for him everywhere?' asked a smartly dressed young woman, clutching the hand of a fretful little girl, whom she addressed crossly. 'Stop fidgeting whilst I'm talking to the gentleman.'

'I haven't seen him anywhere.' Tim took a cursory look around. 'Perhaps he's in the station house or in his office. A porter or the guard may know, that's if you can find one in this crowd.'

'You'd think he'd make an appearance, especially at a time like this,' she remarked, showing her contempt. 'Or some sort of a communication, say a loudspeaker announcement giving likely times of delay. Thanks all the same. Come on, Mandy, stop dragging your feet; haven't I enough to put up with? If you want to see Grandma for Christmas, behave yourself!'

Tim watched, as scolding her tearful charge, she walked away. Wondering what to do, he looked back at the seat he had previously vacated. There was no sign of the old man, so making his way back, he sat down. In an attempt to relax, lighting up a cigarette and inhaling, he sat revelling in a semi-soporific state, a state short-lived, when jerked back to reality by the sound of angry voices. The station master had appeared, apparently being set upon by a number of individuals, their voices raised, pointing to the empty line. The harassed man, shaking his head in despair, said he was none the wiser but would keep them informed. This apparently not good enough for some, a group haranguing and pestering him sent him off in a huff. Some time later, to return in a better frame of mind, the station master told them that there was a problem on the line due to a massive fall of snow causing a blockage, this leaving all and sundry with no option but to spend the night in the waiting room.

Sometime during the night Tim woke up, cold and aching all over, somewhat bewildered by his strange surroundings. He became aware of shadowy figures and heard a sound of snoring, with some lying prostrate and others in the land of nod.

In the early hours, the grey light of dawn creeping under the door with rays of light through the window panes, penetrating even the darkest interior, rubbing the condensation from the glass and looking out, glad of his thick army socks, he tiptoed to the door, once there, gently prising it open.

Outside in the cold, frosty air, pulling on his boots, tightening the belt of his coat and shouldering his kitbag, he crunched his way along the snowy track past the ticket office and out onto the road.

*

It had stopped snowing. As trudging on, with no one in sight, at first he experienced an eerie silence, eventually broken with the sky gradually lightening and the chirping of birds. He was to find himself in another world, a world with beams of street lights picking out shapes of snowdrifts lining each side of the road.

As others, he trudged along, making his way on foot, past abandoned vehicles, his army boots crunching in the snow, the sound of gritters music to his ears. Here and there the coloured lights on a Christmas tree framed in a window gave light relief to an otherwise forbidding landscape, and an intensely cold one. Christmas Day not far away, and no one knowing he was coming home, how surprised they would be, he thought as stopping in his tracks, with the sound of church bells.

He trudged on. In the distance, on seeing the church, its stained-glass windows shedding light, an illuminated star on its steeple, he stopped for a while to catch his breath.

His fingers tingling with the cold – for bitter that it was, it had penetrated his gloves – joining a group of people, he went wearily on his way.

On and on he trudged; a cluster of shops responding to a demand for late-night shopping, their windows adorned with extravaganza, beckoning him, as drawing near, with a thought of presents.

A box of chocolates for Amelia perhaps, by a way of thank you for the way she had and was still looking after Ma? When thinking of Ma, he felt a tinge of sadness. A dark thought occurred. What if she didn't even recognise him? At this time of year when everyone was entering into the spirit of Christmas, such an occasion may serve to confuse her even more.

*

Malcolm had had a sleepless night, twisting and turning in the grey light of dawn, his tortured mind switching from images of Marjorie to those of his adopted parents and then to memories of a drunken father and a mother afraid in a time of crisis and

116

unable to cope. The imagery of the latter, having clearly played a large role in his early development in forming his personality, had certainly been instrumental in creating an inability to accept rejection. To face the fact that any woman he may fancy may not necessarily be attracted to him might not have occurred to him. He was to find no solace in sleep, switching on the bedside light and picking up his wristwatch, somewhat relieved to find the time, eight o'clock.

On opening the window to get some fresh air a light, chilly breeze ruffled the curtains, leaning out over the sill, he looked down at the street below. Not a soul in sight, a quiet wintry scene, the little market town, cushioned in snow, now gradually thawing, icy droplets trickling down narrow channels leading off rooftops and roadsides, here and there a lighted window, a warm glow in an otherwise bleak landscape.

Drawing back from the window, in a corner his eyes alighted on the unwrapped presents he'd recently purchased on an impulse, a sight to him now meaningless and without foundation. Restless, feeling like a caged animal, he suddenly experienced an overwhelming desire to be free, to wander aimlessly. Urged on, he dressed, leaving the room quietly, taking care not to wake Oliver, whose snores could be clearly heard through the paper-thin walls.

Downstairs in the hall he hesitated, his heart missing a beat on hearing a clatter of crockery coming from the direction of a back room and seeing a door ajar leading into the landlady's kitchen. Today of all days he didn't want to see her, but wished to be left alone. Quietly making for the front door he let himself out.

Standing outside on the pavement, the wind changing direction, for the first time he could hear the peal of church bells echoing over the town and the countryside.

The very next moment, bracing himself, head bent with no particular direction in mind, he quickened his pace.

Overhead a weak sun dodging in an out amongst the clouds in an attempt to make an impression, on breaking through, cast rays of sunshine on rooftops of darkened buildings, alleyways and streets. Malcolm, feeling invigorated, chose not to think but observe; in the distance, his curiosity aroused on seeing a figure. Drawing closer, he perceived it to be that of a soldier, and a very tired one, judging by his body language.

Unaware, that he had become a subject of interest, Tim stopped, and heaving the heavy kitbag off his shoulders onto the roadside, paused for a breath. He longed to sit down, but could find nowhere to sit, so resolutely brushing the snow off his greatcoat and attempting to dislodge chunks of ice attached to his boots, was bending down to shoulder his heavy load again, when he became aware of a presence. On looking up he was to see, standing in front of him, a dark-haired man about his own age, eyeing him with some concern.

Chapter 26

'Mr Taylor says we can go early, Rube. He told me to tell you.' Jill tapped her on the shoulder.

'What now?' Ruby looked up from what she was doing. She glanced at her wristwatch. 'But it's only quarter to three.' She frowned. 'Are you sure, we don't want to get into trouble just before Christmas, do we?'

Jill, vivacious and popular, with her devil-may-care attitude having worked in Woolworths for a number of years, had taken Ruby under her wing.

Slightly older than Ruby and stylish with her newly bleached hair, cut in a bob, she eyed Ruby contemptuously, retorting, 'Rube you worry too much, live a little. It's Christmas! I'm going to look up that new boutique in the square; I've been meaning to for a long time.' Her face lighting up at the thought, she said, 'The girls tell me they've got some fab miniskirts in the window.' She closed her eyes, 'I can't wait to try one on – with a nice sparkly top and a pair of high heels, I'll feel a million dollars. What about you Rube, got something special?'

Ruby, somewhat out her depth, vaguely rejoined, 'What? … Me, I haven't thought about it.'

Jill, pulling on her coat and impatient with Ruby's lack of interest, reiterated, 'I'm going without you, if you don't stop mucking about. Come on, grab your coat, let's go.'

With a backward glance, Ruby, having seen Mr Taylor hovering in the background with a congenial look on his face, picked up her coat. 'Oh, I suppose it's alright,' she said.

Ruby, pulling on her gloves on leaving the shop, together with Jill picked her way across compact ridges of snow piled up and formed by a snowplough in an attempt to clear a passage. Wearied by Jill's incessant banter, she disassociated herself, dreamingly musing, for it had been a long and tiring day. Her curiosity was aroused when once or twice she caught a glimpse of the soldier, only to lose sight of him again in the crowded store. In that short time, he had captured her imagination. Who was he? A couple of times, on looking up, she'd found him watching her, his handsome face breaking into a smile as, blushing, she'd met his gaze.

'Did you hear me? ... Rube, I'm talking to you!'

Jerked back to reality, Ruby, aware of Jill's exasperation, said, 'I'm sorry, I'm not much company am I?' Having said this, struck by a thought, putting her hand to her mouth, she gasped.

'What now Rube, what's the matter?' Jill, slightly concerned, stopped in her tracks. 'Come on, snap out of it, we'll walk down to the square together. I for one don't want to hang around here: it's freezing.'

'No, I'd better get back. James will be locked out. I forgot to give him a door key and Ma and Da won't be home from work. I can't leave him out in the cold.'

'So that's what it's all about.' Jill sighed. Shrugging her shoulders, she said, 'You'd best run along and see to it. I'm off, see you tomorrow.'

Alone and exasperated, mostly with her own lack of foresight, Ruby, waving, watched Jill's diminishing figure until out of sight. There was nothing else she could do but make her way to the hospital in the hope of catching James before he left. Ruby, feeling blue with the cold, fastening the top button of her coat, pulled up her collar.

She had not gone far when she caught sight of James in the distance coming towards her, Dog trailing behind him. Trying to attract his attention, she waved her hand, but he didn't respond. Surprised, she glanced at her watch, to find it was only four o'clock. *Where was he going?* she wondered, *had he been to the hospital as he promised he would, and why was he with Dog?* Drawing abreast, she cried, 'Didn't you see me?' James' guarded expression prompted her to add, 'What's wrong, what have you done now? Why is that bit of rope hanging from Dog's collar?'

'It's 'e's fault, it ain't mine.' James eyed Dog, who was laying down, his nose on paws, his ears flattening when picking up the vibes. 'I've done nothin', 'onest!'

'What about Dog?'

''E's ... 'e's ...'

'Come on, James, spit it out.'

''E broke free, got into the hospital, followed me an' ...' James, overcome, unable to finish the sentence, broke down sobbing uncontrollably.

Ruby, perturbed at his distress, drawing him to her, put her arm around his shoulders. 'Calm down, come home with me and tell me all about it.' Her voice gentle and reassuring, taking out a handkerchief, she wiped his tear-stained face.

This evoked a strong reaction from James, 'Don't 'e do that, I ain't a babe.'

Ungraciously and half-heartedly, tagging behind, he followed Ruby home, Dog shadowing.

In the warm confines of the back kitchen, Ruby watched in a quandary as James, having scrambled unceremoniously up on a high stool, sat looking out the window.

'What's wrong, what is so terribly wrong?' she cried, trying to evoke a reaction.

For a moment, silence, then James, twisting around on the stool and looking at her for the first time, unflinchingly and emphatically said, 'It was Dog's fault.'

Dog, lying near to the door, on hearing his name, snuffling in recognition, raised his head. On looking at James, he flattened his ears, his tail thumping on the tiles half-heartedly on hearing his voice: 'I 'ate you ... go away and don't 'e come back!'

'What happened?' Ruby, all ears, stepped a little closer.

''E followed me up to 'er room.'

'Marj's room?'

James, nodding his head, gasped, 'An'... an' they all turned up, I heard 'em coming.'

'Who?' Ruby, baffled by such intensity, was beginning to fear the worst.

'Marj's Ma, Da and 'er Gran ... so I hid Dog.'

'Where?'

'Under Marj's bed.'

'What!' Ruby could hardly believe her ears. 'Whatever were you thinking of? Go and clean yourself up, you're coming with me to the hospital to apologise.'

'What, right now? Us 'ave only jist come home.'

'Yes, right now, and get a move on.'

'But, I can't cos ...'

'No more excuses, you do as you're told.' Ruby frowned. 'I was beginning to feel so proud of you and now you've let me down, haven't you?'

'I told 'e it wasn't me fault, it ...'

'Never mind that, did you hear what I said? Go and get ready; we're going to the hospital and we're not taking that dog.'

*

'I'll put the flowers in water fer 'e, Mary.' Amelia frowned, 'What's happened to James, I didn't see 'im go?'

'I might 'ave known 'e'd make off when our backs were turned with that dog. Goodness knows what 'e's up to now.' Mary, her eyes darting around a whitewashed room smelling of carbolic soap, as if in a futile attempt to catch sight of him, pursed her lips.

'It's the dog I'm worried about – I hope it's now under control,' said the nurse. Followed by the orderly, intent on her duties, she was now making for the door. 'Do ring, should you need any assistance.'

'I'd better be on my way too,' said the fair-haired girl, who up until now had a tendency to linger. 'You needn't worry about Charlie, he's an old softie and wouldn't harm anyone.' She glanced at her watch. 'I'll have to go. I'm visiting ...'

'Jist afore 'e goes, Miss.' Amelia, in an attempt to glean information, forestalled her. ''E's the kennel maid from the pound, ain't 'e?'

'Yes, for my sins I've been working there for a number of years. My name is Tammy.' Her face lighting up, the kennel maid smiled, 'It's hard work, but they're worth it.'

'No doubt 'e'll know 'bout the dog's history?'

Mary squeezing Marjorie's hand prompted her to comment, 'But fer that dog, where would I be? Me mind's playin' tricks? It's sort of familiar, it's as if …'

'Yes?' Amelia, raising an enquiring eyebrow, moved closer to the bed.

Marjorie sighed. Pushing her hair away from her forehead, she said, 'As if from some other place, some other time. Do 'e think it's come back to haunt me?'

'Don't worry yer little head, 'tis naught but a bad dream.' Mary, catching hold of her hand, squeezed it again. 'T'will go away, 'e'll see.'

'But wot if it ain't a dream, wot if …' Marjorie increased her grip.

'If it's any help, I will tell you Charlie's history, but not now, I'm late already and my friend, who's recovering from a serious illness, looks forward to my visits.' Tammy broke the ensuing silence. 'I'm so sorry, I would have else.'

'Don't 'e fret, you run along.' Amelia, taking the bunch of flowers out of the vase, handed them to her. 'And take 'em with 'e. Marj won't mind, t'will cheer yer friend up.'

Tammy, touched by her generosity, said. 'You shouldn't have!' The next moment, on opening the door to reveal two figures, stepping back, she exclaimed. 'I didn't know anyone was out there. Why, it's James. Where's Charlie?'

'I'm James' sister; we've left the dog at home.' Ruby cast a baleful look at James hovering in the doorway. 'I've brought James to apologise.'

'I see. By the way, my name's Tammy. It's nice to have met you all, but I really must be on my way.'

The door closing behind her, Ruby and James approached the bedside, James fully expecting to find Marjorie badly injured or at worst dead.

'Hello Ruby, 'ow nice to see 'e.' Marjorie, propped up in bed, smiled at her. Puzzled by the expression on James' face, she asked, 'Wot's wrong wi' 'im?'

James could hardly believe his eyes; Ruby, also taken completely by surprise, experienced mixed emotions, those of joy and relief. On seeing James' reaction, she could understand Marjorie's amazement. Standing there perfectly still, his eyes trancelike as if seeing a ghost, he looked so comical, a sight evoking in her a strong tendency to laugh, an emotion to be held in check.

Flustered, blushing and embarrassed, aware of being the centre of attention, he stammered, 'I … I thought 'e might've bin dead.'

'Why would you have thought that?' Ruby, bewildered by this unexpected revelation, gasped.

'Cos … of Dog?'

'What about Dog?' demanded Ruby, her tone hardening as losing patience.

Feeling sorry for James, Amelia, at that moment coming to his rescue, as giving an account of the dog's previous activities when emerging from underneath the bed, how boisterous and out of control when evading capture, it had been instrumental in the re-awakening and the cause of Marjorie's full recovery.

Ruby's eyes grew bigger as listening, now and then glancing at James, her mouth set in a hard line. Unable to meet her questioning look, he looked away.

Not so Charles. Charles, who all this time had been sitting in his wheelchair by the window and hadn't up until now said much, was heard to comment, 'Don't 'e be too hard on the boy, it ain't entirely 'e's fault. The dog has been the making of 'im.'

Encouraged by his support, James rallied. Addressing Charles, he remarked, 'I don't know, sometimes I hates 'im and then I loves 'im, don't I Rube?' Confused and perplexed, he looked enquiringly at Ruby for some sort of response, finding none.

Marjorie, who for quite a while had been observing James floundering with futile explanations, all of which were leaving no impact on a sister who had heard them all before, was beginning to feel a certain amount of compassion for the troubled ten year old. From her vantage point and looking directly at Ruby, she said, 'Don't you see, if it hadn't been for the dog, I may never have recovered? It's a miracle. One could say "God works in mysterious ways".' Clutching the coverlet and beckoning to James, her face wreathed in smiles, she coaxed, 'Come over here an' stand by the bed, I want to thank 'e. You're a good boy really an' your heart's in the right place.'

Ruby, taken aback with such an unexpected reaction, at first nonchalant and unforgiving, then mellowing, allowed her face to break into a smile.

For a while, there remained an embarrassed silence, each person searching for the appropriate words, but finding none, a breakdown of communication, an unfortunate silence, broken only by Charles who, effortlessly propelling his wheelchair closer to the window and peering out, exclaimed, ''Tis snowin'!'

True enough, from a leaden sky, snowflakes were falling, settling on rooftops, smoke spiralling from myriad chimneys set against a backdrop of distant hills, fringed with a stark outline of trees.

Joining Charles at the windowsill, Amelia looked down into a paved courtyard peppered with snow. 'Us best be off, wi' the weather closin' in.' Speaking from experience, when picturing in her mind unrelenting banks of snow, quaking inwardly, she turned to Ruby and James. 'An' I advise 'e to do the same, afore it gits dark.'

Ruby nodded in agreement. Well aware of worsening conditions, with one glance at the darkening skies and thoughts of a potential snow storm, she had known it was time to go.

'Ssss … shh,' Amelia, putting her hand to her mouth at that moment, exclaimed, 'Listen, what's that? I 'eard something, it sounded like …'

'Like carol singers; yes I heard 'em, but only jist.' Marjorie, sitting up in bed, listened intently.

'Singing in the square, I expect – the same as last year. You never know, they may come this way.' Glancing at a solemn-faced James in an attempt to gain his attention, Ruby cried, 'Can you hear what they're singing, James?'

Shaken out of his apathy, James, giving his sister a cursory look, stammered, 'Silent … Silent Night, 'Oly Night.' Flustered, still smarting from her intolerant attitude and quite suspicious of her change of heart, wondering how long it would last, he didn't know what to think.

''Tis Christmas! Wot's the matter with 'e?' Amelia, her good-natured face lighting up, cried, ''E oughta be happy, not sad. Best us be making tracks with the weather worsenin', don' 'e think?'

''Er's right, you know: us best be goin' afore it closes in.' Charles, setting his wheelchair in motion, his hands on the wheels, started steering towards the door. 'An' a Merry Christmas be 'ad by all.'

'Will 'e stop natterin'!' Amelia by the window, wiping away the condensation with the edge of her cuff, peered out. ''Tis black as pitch – can't see anything but them street lights …'

'Then what's 'e on about?' Charles asked, stopping in his tracks, 'If 'e can't see anything?'

'Can't 'e hear it?' Each of them, curious, crowded around the window, James with his nose pressed against the windowpane. At first indistinct and then nearing, as if the volume of a giant radio had been turned up, the strains of old familiar carols soon could be heard ringing out in the courtyard below.

'I told you so,' Ruby, moving closer to the window, nudged James gently aside. 'But I'm blowed if I can see anything.'

'I see's 'em!' James, having maintained his foothold, had caught a glimpse.

'Where?' Ruby scanned a dark expanse.

'There, can 'e see 'em now?' James cried, pointing to the wrought iron gates, through which figures could be seen emerging, past old stone walls fringed with white, into a courtyard, barely visible in the still, dark night. There they stopped, faces lifted, their voices in unison, ringing out in a cold and frosty atmosphere, Christmas lanterns swaying, casting myriad patterns over cobbles flecked with snow.

Marjorie, watching those gathered at the window, now glad to be on the road to recovery, thought of Malcolm. *Where was he? Why wasn't he here with the rest of her family and friends?* No one had mentioned his name, not even in passing. A dark thought occurred, bringing with it a cold sensation, a feeling of neglect. *Didn't he care, didn't their time together mean anything, especially when sharing such a traumatic experience, and in such a way?*

Initially happy at the prospect of being back home again in the bosom of the family, a solitary tear ran down her cheek as the door closed behind them.

Chapter 27

Maureen was looking forward to seeing her family and friends at the get-together at Christmas. Unlike Malcolm, she came from a big family with brothers and sisters, and with her sparkling personality had quite a lot of friends, so was never short of company. At first drawn to Malcolm's good looks, but later disenchanted by his serious outlook on life and an inability to loosen up, she was losing interest.

'Have you got all your presents?' she asked him. 'It won't be long now before closing, and Christmas soon over, in the New Year, with the sales, we'll be run off our feet.' She pulled a face.

'I've been wondering what to do about Marjorie; what do you think?' Malcolm, having hardly heard a word she said, raised an enquiring eyebrow.

'For a present? I wouldn't know. She's not aware of the season is she?'

Malcolm looked downcast. Maureen, placing a reassuring hand on his shoulder, with an inexplicable surge of emotion, there and then, was compelled to say, 'How about a drink and a bar snack in the pub at lunchtime?'

Taking her by surprise, and seemingly knocking the wind out of her sails, he gasped, 'Why not, after all it is Christmas.'

She laughed, carried away with his enthusiasm. But trudging through the snow on their way to the pub, their conversation not so spontaneous, Malcolm not his usual self, she asked, 'Is anything wrong?' puzzled by his attitude.

'Nothing more than usual,' avoiding eye contact he answered, terse and to the point.

'Are you sure?' she asked, feeling slightly inadequate. 'If there's anything I can do?'

'No, nothing,' his voice at first somewhat restrained, then lightening up, he cried, 'Come on, it's Christmas isn't it? Let's enjoy it.'

*

In the smoky atmosphere of the Lion's Lair, Maureen, sitting on a bar stool nursing a gin and tonic, having become aware of Malcolm's changing demeanour was beginning to feel ill at ease. Twisting the signet ring on her finger, she blushed with him appraising her in a manner she found disconcerting.

I hope he's not getting the wrong idea, she thought, *if so, I should only blame myself, but he looked so down in the mouth.* With a reflex action, she crossed her legs, a movement not escaping his notice. *What a pity,* she thought, *that through a misunderstanding, a working relationship such as ours, which had always been so compatible, should be spoilt in this way.*

'You're very quiet Maureen; didn't you like your drink?' Malcolm asked, aware of her discomfort. Eager to please, he suggested, 'Perhaps you'd like another?'

The combined desire of a drink enabling her to relax and to be free of his scrutiny, if only for a moment, prompted her to say, 'Oh, yes please.'

Left alone, in a detached frame of mind, Maureen, toying with her drink, wondered what to say to Malcolm to put the record straight. *What a mess ... What a tangled web,* she thought. Looking up she spotted Malcolm further along the bar talking to Barry from the plant department, who had just come in. For a while unaware of her scrutiny, deep in conversation, and then prompted by something one of them had said, both looked in her direction. Barry, having caught her eye, clapped Malcolm on the back when passing some sort of remark.

Maureen, as if frozen to the spot, watched them making their way towards her, Barry with a sardonic expression on his face, beckoning Malcolm. *If only the ground would open and swallow me up,* she thought.

'You're a dark horse, Maureen!' Barry exclaimed, laughing at her with his eyes. 'Right under my nose, too.'

The colour rushing to her cheeks, fixing Malcolm with a piecing look, she retorted, 'I wish I'd never come.'

Barry, clearing his throat, aware of an atmosphere of restraint, tried to bluff his way out of an embarrassing situation. 'I'm sorry if I've upset the applecart,' he said, after an awkward pause. 'I've got to be going anyway – see you around sometime, maybe.'

As soon as he had gone, Maureen, swinging around on the bar stool, confronted Malcolm. Enraged and indignant, she glared at him. 'How could you!' she cried, 'How could you make such a fool of me?'

'But I thought …' his sentence was cut short by her angry reaction.

'You made me feel cheap and nasty! I shall be a laughing stock.' Completely out of his depth, perplexed and bewildered, Malcolm turned away.

Her protests attracted a number of individuals gathered around the bar, some inebriated, others sniggering at her outburst. The shrill voice of a woman in a tight-knit group close by could be clearly heard, 'Perhaps she's not getting enough!' a comment followed by guffaws.

'Take no notice of them.' Malcolm, embarrassed and searching desperately for the right words, said, 'We haven't had our bar snack yet, what do you fancy?'

'Nothing from you!' Maureen, now the centre of attention, giving vent to her emotions, ranted on, 'I've never been so humiliated in my life!' With that, jumping off the stool, she flounced out, leaving Malcolm to face the music.

*

Back in the gift shop, one could only describe the rest of the afternoon as a nightmare, a nightmare of indifference. So near and yet so far, Malcolm occasionally caught a glimpse of her profile, then her face, on it a wooden expression, so unapproachable, revealing nothing. The sight filled him with an aching despondency. If only he could right the wrong, but now the barriers were up, their long-term working friendship broken, and all because of a foolish whim on his part. Was it though? Of course it was, not a glimmer of hope – any chance of any sort of a relationship over. With so much suspicion, she saw it a betrayal.

The afternoon dragged on, each of them in their own way putting on a front for those around them, speaking to each other only when necessary and then with a polite, cool indifference.

*

The snowy, bleak landscape seemed to mirror Malcolm's mood as on reaching the flat, cold, hungry and humiliated, he just wanted to be alone. He wished only to sit down and think, to unravel his tangled emotions, to bring some semblance of order into a life that seemed to be going nowhere.

Malcolm, letting himself in, found a light on in the hallway, but no one there. Puzzled, as one of the landlady's golden rules was never to waste electricity, he stood there for a moment, listening intently. Then he called her name, thinking perhaps she was out the back and couldn't hear him. For a time all was quiet, then he heard movements in the flat upstairs. He switched off the light. Who could it be? Strange, he thought, for Oliver was working late.

Every fibre of his being alert, preparing for the worst, Malcolm was just about to go up the stairs when the flat door swung open, revealing Oliver. He glanced down at Malcolm standing in the dim hallway, for a moment speechless, he then said, 'I'm glad I've caught you, I've got to get back … I'm afraid I've some bad news.' He held out a telegram which had already been slit open – a sight filling Malcolm with a mixture of annoyance and foreboding.

'I'm sorry about that.' Oliver, feeling sensitive when aware of Malcolm's reaction, tried to explain, saying, 'I opened it by mistake … I didn't mean to pry, but I'm afraid I've read it. It's your parents, they're …'

Without paying any attention to Oliver's explanation, Malcolm literally snatched it from him. He stood there momentarily numb and oblivious to his surroundings, with the words penetrating his brain, "I regret to inform you that your parents have been killed in a plane crash."

Chapter 28

It had stopped snowing. A weak sun was shining down on a snow-trodden road, now churned up, a dirty greyish colour, particles melting, gurgling down drains, revealing large areas of wet tarmac – to many after the freeze, a welcomed sight.

With glimpses of the sun, Malcolm, on reaching the bus stop, joined the end of a rather straggly queue. As if in a daze for a while he stood there, deep in thought, his hands in his pockets, then pulling the envelope out of his coat, he assimilated its contents.

> Dear Sir,
> We are pleased to inform you that you are the sole beneficiary of the estate of Mr and Mrs Nathanial Knight.
> In order to discuss the matter, please attend this office at 10 a.m. on Thursday, 20th December.
> Yours faithfully,
>
> Rupert Potter

Seated in the bus, Malcolm stared uncomprehendingly out of the window at the passing countryside. At first shocked by the news, by the suddenness, the finality of a change of circumstances, now, to his surprise, he felt nothing but an overwhelming feeling of relief. Searching his heart, he knew he had never loved them – there had been a coldness, an indefinable bridge between him and his parents, one which from his earliest childhood he had felt unable to cross. Consequently, in no time their relationship soured; with a breakdown of communication, they had each gone their separate ways.

The bus, with a hiss of air brakes, pulled up in the town

square. A number of passengers having alighted, attracted by a garlanded Christmas tree decked with coloured lights in its centre, made a beeline towards it. The square was not so busy, most people now intent on getting last-minute presents or Christmas hampers hopefully filled to the brim with favourite wines, spirits, puddings, cakes, sweets and biscuits, leaving the vegetables and poultry until the last moment. Malcolm, detaching himself from the hustle and bustle, making his way away from the lighted shops and turning a corner, found himself in a back lane.

He had had no reason to set foot in Friars Lane before and had not been aware of its existence until now. Tucked away from sight, with its Dickensian silvery-grey atmosphere and old stone cottages, it was a step back in time. Residues of snow added to the magic, lining the windowsills of quaint little shops built in a higgledy-piggledy manner bordering the narrow cobblestone lane on which he trod. Holly wreaths here and there adorned doors with scrubbed steps, highly polished brass name plates, door knockers and door stops. A fleeting sun appearing from behind a cloud lit up leaded windows and mysterious alleyways running off.

'And a Merry Christmas to you,' a butcher, his ruddy face wreathed in smiles, calling out to Malcolm as passing by, was standing in front of his shop. His shirt sleeves rolled up, he was wearing a striped apron and a straw boater, bedecked with holly. 'And a Happy New Year!' he cried, doffing his boater.

Malcolm, mustering up a smile, barely looked at the geese and un-plucked turkeys hanging from steel hooks, or the cuts of lamb, pork, beef or venison. Braces of pheasant, all artistically arranged on marble slabs, with packets of sage and onion, thyme, jars of sauces, tins of gravy to tempt the palate … to him all these of little significance, merely a festive display, only succeeding in exacerbating an acute feeling of loneliness, a feeling of being unwanted with no incentive or aim. Currently, in this state of mind, he glanced at his watch. It was ten to ten; at least he wasn't late for his appointment.

A woman looked up as he approached the offices of Potter, Potter & Broadbent, Solicitors & Commissioners of Oaths. Perspiring, she had been cleaning the brass, and was screwing the top back on a tin of Brasso. After rising awkwardly to her feet, she smiled. 'Am I in your way? I shall be going inside any moment myself, thank God, it's getting rather parky out here.'

Once inside the door, Malcolm, his eyes gradually adjusting, found himself in the dim interior of a hallway smelling of polish. On hearing the clatter of a typewriter coming from within the direction of a door on the left, boldly marked, "Reception, Please Enter", he tried the handle. The door swinging open, he stepped into a fairly large room.

An elderly woman, her iron-grey hair pulled back in a bun, was sitting at a desk facing the window, laboriously typing away. Totally unaware of his presence, he coughed. Startled, she swivelled around on her chair. Observing him over horn-rimmed glasses, she managed a smile, saying, 'Mr Knight, Mr Malcolm Knight? You have an appointment with Mr Rupert at 10 a.m. He won't be long; he's with a client at the moment. Please take a seat.'

Malcolm, observing his surroundings, was to find that like the hall, the light in the room was dim, remedied by a small chandelier, which to him seemed somewhat out of place hanging from the centre of the low, wood-beam ceiling. There were also a number of filing cabinets in an alcove by the leaded window, through which he could just see glimpses of the lane outside. In another corner, a glass cabinet stacked with books caught his eye, as did a large open fireplace with a heavy timber mantelpiece.

It was not long before he heard a distant murmur of voices, the slamming of doors, footsteps echoing along the passageway, then silence was broken as the Bakelite telephone shrilled on its stand. Getting up in response, the receptionist announced rather haughtily, 'Mr Rupert will see you now, please follow me.'

To begin with, Malcolm was not at all impressed with Mr Rupert, but he was soon to find that he was not a man to be trifled with. He wouldn't suffer fools. Although not very formidable in appearance, he was shrewd and pulled no punches.

A balding, bespectacled, somewhat insignificant man ensconced in his inner sanctum, seated behind an enormous mahogany desk littered with a number of books, pens, pencils, rubbers and rulers, documents and typewritten letters presumably awaiting his signature, he barely looked up. Hanging on the wall behind him was a large portrait, presumably that of an ancestor standing in characteristic pose, a very forceful looking gentleman with a handlebar moustache and stern eyes, his hand resting on a terrestrial globe. Adjacent, a number of certificates of academic qualifications; to the right a large, leaded window, similar to that of the room he had just left, this looking out onto a small courtyard dappled in sunlight.

The lawyer, undeterred by his presence, taking his time examining a document, on looking up and apologising for keeping Malcolm waiting, indicated a chair.

Malcolm, handing him the letter as a means of introduction, watched Mr Rupert as, scanning it, he said, mostly to himself, 'Knight … Knight, now where did I put that file … Oh, yes, of course, it's in the cabinet.' On jumping up, he drew it out. With his hand hovering over the telephone, he then said courteously, 'Would you like tea or coffee?'

'No thank you,' Malcolm replied, for behind his mask of politeness was the desire to get the whole tedious business over and out of the way.

The lawyer, sitting well back in his chair, without saying anything for a few seconds, held Martin in his gaze, an experience he found disconcerting. Then, suddenly finding his voice said, 'I think my letter to you was quite self-explanatory, simply that you are the sole beneficiary of the estate. The will has to go though probate, and of course, I shall need to see some proof of identity. Your stepfather left his brother, Richard, as executor. Unfortunately, he and his wife too were with …'

'My stepfather?' Malcolm queried, interrupting the lawyer's flow, his mind suddenly in turmoil.

Mr Rupert, looking at him long and hard, then with a certain amount of amazement, said, 'But surely they told you.'

Feeling at a disadvantage by the revelation, and inwardly angry, conscious of the lawyer's scrutiny, Malcolm, humbling himself, simply said, 'No, but it explains a lot.'

Hard-boiled as he was, the lawyer couldn't help but feel a certain amount of compassion for the young man, and continuing as if nothing had happened from where he had left off, said, 'Now where was I? Oh, yes … with them on the plane, at the time, so were also killed. But we will relieve you of any needless worry. Our firm will now attend to all necessary business and as the will is very simple, everything should be quite straight forward.' Then, clearing his throat and glancing up at the wall clock, Mr Rupert said, 'Just one more thing.' On opening up the file, and drawing out a small envelope, he said, 'I have in my possession a letter of which I have been instructed to hand to you in the event of your adopted parent's deaths.' Rising in a rather ungainly manner from behind his desk, after rummaging in the file, he handed over the letter, Malcolm, overshadowed with a feeling of foreboding, taking it from him. The appointment at an end, he stood up. The lawyer, with a fleeting smile, stretched out his hand, a firm handshake once again reassuring Malcolm of his commitment – then speaking into an intercom in a loud and clear voice, 'Miss Pryor, will you see Mr Knight out.'

Once again outside in the lane, clutching the envelope, Malcolm, pausing for a moment, could see in the distance the butcher's shop, its lighted front with its tempting produce. He could hear the butcher's voice, with a number of people in a queue jostling for attention. All of them happy and eager, although tired, joking and laughing with the coming of Christmas, everything normal as it should be, but for him. Would normality for him, he wondered, be just an illusion?

Chapter 29

It was getting dark, the air chilly, as Malcolm, on reaching his lodgings, let himself in. The light in the hall was on, but although no one about, it was evident that his landlady was in, for he could hear the strains of a radio issuing from the back room as climbing the stairs. The flat was empty, as he knew it would be. Oliver, taking a well deserved break, was out for the evening with friends, taking part in a snooker match at the Lion's Lair.

He discarded the envelope he had knowingly clutched since leaving the lawyer's office onto a small coffee table near to the window. With a view to lighting the electric fire, having run out of coins, he emptied his purse to feed the meter. This done, he switched on the fire, holding out his hands to savour the warmth from its bars. Tired and hungry, slipping out of his coat, he foraged in the refrigerator for any leftovers, fully aware that he needed to restock his diminishing supply for himself as well as for Oliver, who generally accompanied him on the odd occasion, other than that leaving most of the shopping to him. Relieved on finding some eggs and a small piece of cheddar, Malcolm quickly whipped up an omelette, and sprinkling it with grated cheese, washed it down with a glass of wine. Now refreshed, he turned his attention to the window and to the coffee table on which lay the letter. He switched on the lamp, flooding the room with light, as crossing to the table with bottle and glass, he laid them down. Stretching over to draw the curtains closed, Malcolm stopped for a time, taking in the view, before shutting out the night. At any other time, he would have marvelled at the sight, at the magic of a star-studded sky with a full moon suspended in space, lighting up a wintry landscape blanketed in snow. Nevertheless, blind to its beauty, pulling the curtains across, he turned away, his curiosity aroused, drawn again to the unopened letter within his reach.

*

Malcolm was totally unprepared for the revelations disclosed. Detached but transfixed as the strands of his childhood were unravelled, the mysteries clarified, for the first time finding out the reasons for the attitudes of those around him, those upon whom he had been so dependant and incapable of understanding.

Pouring himself a glass of wine and holding it up against the light, toying with its liquid contents as swirling it around, then drinking it down in one go, he replaced the empty glass on the table. With a shaking hand, he picked up and slit open the envelope.

At first glance, the familiar spidery writing only filled him with contempt, this and other emotions in due course coming to the surface, as reading the following:

> Dear Malcolm,
> Should anything happen to us, knowing well things couldn't have been easy for you, we feel you are entitled to some sort of explanation.

'Not easy? That's putting it mildly … what explanation?' Malcolm, on the point of tearing up the letter, changed his mind.

> A newly born baby, your father not being able to take care or provide for you, you were offered up for adoption.
> A fisherman, his vessel requisitioned in the nineteen forties, along with others, a part of a small but necessary armada, he ferried the wounded and dying away from the Normandy Coast across the Channel to safety in England.
> Haunted and traumatised by images he couldn't forget, not normally a man who was prone to drink, he turned more and more to the bottle for solace, neglecting and leaving your mother with you, as a baby, destitute and unable to cope. On her own and not in the best of health, frail but resourceful,

at times her spirit broken, she gave up the struggle. In those turbulent times, with the threat of war and a possible invasion, deeply depressed, not knowing which way to turn, on an impulse she took an overdose, ending her miserable existence and leaving you at the mercy of your father.

So that's it, Malcolm thought, *my father preferred the bottle to me, and my mother died in the process. Do I really want to know that! Adopted, should I be thankful? I don't think so, not as things have turned out. A plane crash, if you ask me, nothing more than they deserved. Why bother with this?* Lips pursed, a lump in his throat, stepping to the windowsill, pulling back the curtains, seeing only his reflection in the glass, Malcolm's eyes met a black void.

Burning with curiosity, having scooped up the letter, he read on:

And that's where we came in. Jonathan, our own son, was sickly and not strong – not able to have any more children of our own, we adopted you, only some years later to lose him in a tragic accident.

At first we blamed you for playing in the park …

Malcolm, like a caged animal, wearing out the carpet pacing to and fro, to and fro, when visualising long-forgotten faces with unforgiving expressions, raged – *What for? What have I done, nothing except breathe; blame me for what, playing in the park? For what?* Unceremoniously, he flicked over the page.

… one day with your friends. Jonathan, merely a bystander, was encouraged to join in. Aged seven, we had asked you to keep an eye on him, even though at that age, not totally aware of your brother's infirmity.

Although I didn't know it, he wasn't my brother was he? Why should I have had to look after him? Malcolm, his temper rising even more at the thought, fumed. 'And why am I bothering to read this letter, they're only trying to clear their conscience … a bit late now. Still, what now?' he muttered, wiping away smears on his reading glasses.

> That fateful afternoon, a boy carrying a make-shift boat was making his way to the lake to launch it, followed by a jostling group of youngsters eager to join him. Possibly inheriting your father's love of the sea, fascinated, you followed them, unaware of a solitary figure having broken away from the group, wandering perilously close to the water's edge. Too late you realised. Rushed to hospital Jonathan survived, but only for a little while, finally dying of pneumonia. Bitter at the loss, we unfairly blamed you, secretly wishing we had not adopted you.

So that's it, is it? Dropping the letter on the table, Malcolm, slumping into the chair, cradling his head in his hands, wept. Then pulling himself together, picking up the letter, he read on:

> Now, years after and with hindsight, we are aware how unfeeling we were towards you when you were at such a sensitive age – knowing now after all this time, you may not find it in your heart to forgive us. In time we hope you will, and find the kind of happiness you so richly deserve.

> With all our love and affection,
> John and Jane Knight.

'I will,' said Malcolm, pouring himself some wine. He emptied the glass, 'But not with your help.' He crumpled up the letter and tossed it into the nearest ashtray. Pouring himself another glass of wine, he struck a match and watched as the letter writhed in flames, a sight symbolic of his past life; and with the dying down of flames, the charred remains were reminiscent of an end of those times with a new beginning.

Aware of the sound of the church clock striking midnight, sitting there, still holding the empty glass, with a car pulling up and the crunching of tyres on snow, as stationery, its engine still running, he heard Oliver's voice: 'Thanks for bringing me home; I can't wait to tell Malcolm the news.'

What news? Could it be good news, an unexpected start to his new lease of life, to his long-awaited dreams of a newly found freedom?

Not knowing what to expect, Malcolm, opening the flat door, looked down the stairs. Oliver, singularly unaware of his presence, was standing in the hallway fumbling with his door keys. The door creaking open, on looking up and catching sight of Malcolm, he smiled. 'I was looking for my key to the flat,' he explained, 'I thought I'd lost it. You're up late – I thought you'd have been in bed by now.' Malcolm's sober expression striking him as odd, he added, 'Is anything wrong?'

'No, nothing, everything's fine now, just as it should be,' Malcolm answered truthfully.

Puzzled by a reply he couldn't make head or tail of, Oliver shrugged his shoulders and, changing the subject in an attempt to cheer him up, said, 'Anyway, I've got good news, the best. It's Marjorie, she's back in the land of the living.'

Chapter 30

It was on Christmas Eve when Malcolm, making his way down the stairs from his flat, encountered his landlady.

'Going out again?' Mrs Piper raised an enquiring eyebrow.

Looking down at her in response he nodded. On passing her in the darkened hallway, pausing, as surveying him with a critical eye, she said, 'You're looking as thin as a rake. I hope you're not coming down with something – even in this light you look quite pale.'

'Don't worry, I'm alright,' Malcolm, wishing to be free of her scrutiny, turning away, edged towards the door,

Unperturbed by his reticence, catching hold of his sleeve, she cried, 'I could cook you a steak and kidney pie, it wouldn't be a problem.'

Disengaging his sleeve from her grasp, Malcolm slightly embarrassed, mustering up a smile, said, 'No thanks, but it's very kind of you.'

'Well if you're sure, I've a lot to do anyway,' she said as moving away down the passageway. 'My daughter and her family are coming down for Christmas, they should be here any moment.'

Outside, standing on the doorstep, Malcolm feeling a nip in the air, pulled up the collar of his coat. Wishing he'd worn a scarf, without any gloves his hands blue with the cold in his pockets, head bent against the driving snow, he made his way slowly down the road.

The steady snowfall yet again in danger of causing potential chaos, already the snowploughs were out making their ponderous way through streets, where hardly a soul could be seen. With most of the shopping done, many were taking refuge at home, ensconced in front of a blazing fire, this evident with spirals of smoke from innumerable cottage chimneys.

Malcolm, with hindsight, now wished he had brought an umbrella, for at least it would have given his shoulders and head some protection from the snowfall. Even so, undeterred, with an ultimate aim, he ploughed on.

At that moment, unbeknown to Malcolm, James, wearing a woolly hat, mittens knitted by Ruby, a thick coat slightly too big for him and a pair of boots as per his Ma's instructions, was picking his way up the icy garden path, Dog at his heels. His demeanour, gloomy, for having lost contact with most of his friends through frequent visits to the hospital, he was becoming bored and aimless. He tugged at the garden gate. Frozen solid at the base and covered in snow, it refused to budge, barring his way. 'It ain't fair,' he stormed, the watchful Dog, in turn, snuffling in recognition. 'Where's me mates? I can't see 'em anywhere. I've gotta find 'em.' Fired by this thought, when scrambling over the low wall and dropping down on the other side, followed by Dog, panting loudly, his breath clouding the freezing air, he trudged down the road.

Ruby, watching James' from the window with a feeling of dismay, as ripping the mittens he'd scaled the wall. 'Ma, did you know, James has gone out, and in this weather?'

'Yes,' said a voice from the kitchen. 'As long as he's bundled up against the cold, he's best out the way.'

Ruby losing interest, moving away from the sill to the fire-place, in a futile attempt to revive the dying embers in the grate, picked up the coal scuttle. 'I know what you mean. I know; James can be a pain. Anyway, we need some coal. I'll go to the shed and get some before it gets dark.'

*

James, with a grubby handkerchief wiping away moisture currently blinding him from snowflakes, now falling thick and fast, trudged on. On his way, stopping by the wayside, with Dog investigating the mysterious frozen vapour from the sky, he was to catch sight of a lone figure.

Malcolm had not slept at all well, tossing and turning over and over again, analysing the contents of the letter and its implications, his thoughts turning to Marjorie. Did he have any feelings for her? Mixed emotions chasing each other round and round in circles, his mind cluttered with useless information, in a darkened room, with a never-ending night, he was so pleased, on awakening early in the cold light of day, to collect his thoughts, to put them together in some semblance of order. He now felt that his life had come to an impasse, a time when a change of direction was needed, but how and when? Something had to be done! Reassessing his short association with Marjorie, until the time of the accident and her long-term illness, he now knew through his recent misconstrued amorous intentions, and Maureen's consequent rebuttal, that he was not ready for a long-term association. But to tell Marjorie of his doubts at a time like this? When after a miraculous recovery, back in the bosom of the family she loved?

Absorbed and preoccupied, weighed down with such notions, Malcolm did not know that a forthcoming brief encounter would give him cause for thought, but in a different direction.

Head down, shielding his face against driving snow impeding his progress, he slowly made his way, until shaken from his reverie by a familiar voice.

'Ain't 'e Marj's friend?'

James, his eyes lighting up on meeting up with him, was standing in front of him. His woolly hat pulled over his ears, sporting an oversized overcoat, gloves and wellies, he cried, 'Where be goin'? 'E be goin' the wrong way, if 'e be goin' to the square.'

'I was on my way to the railway station.' A smile played around Malcolm's lips, as thinking of the boy's audacity.

'Goin' away?'

'No James, just looking up the timetables.'

With this response, James momentarily lost for words.

Breaking the silence, Malcolm asked, 'Where are you off to then?'

'On me way to the square wi' Dog. I gets bored at 'ome, likes to be on me own wi Dog, then I can do what I wants, see.' His eyes narrowing, he asked, ''E ain't goin' away is 'e?'

'Not at the moment.' Malcolm, in a lighter frame of mind, with a change of heart, to James' delight, said, 'Perhaps I'll walk with you to the square instead, would you like that?'

James, nodding his head, smiled, Dog, up from his haunches, shaking himself vigorously.

Together they plodded along, Malcolm still wishing he had brought his umbrella with snowflakes falling relentlessly, but pleased with James' company. Silent since meeting James, Malcolm was now thinking of Marjorie and Christmas, having got no presents for her or her family.

As if picking up on his train of thought, James said, ''Er's nice, ain't 'er?'

'Who?'

'Marj.'

'What makes you say that?'

'Cos 'er understands us, more than Rube.'

It was cold, the traffic again at a standstill, as trudging along with Dog running here and there, occasionally barking and playing in the snow, James gradually unburdened himself. Childlike he would reveal a side of Marjorie's character Malcolm had quite forgotten, and a facet of himself, which he had to admit he didn't like.

She had certainly left an impression on James, "through the mouths of babes" he had told him how she understood and forgave him for the incident with the dog, irrespectively of how things may have turned out. Things that Ruby may have said wouldn't have beared thinking about.

Nearing the square, James subdued with sights and sounds and thoughts of his own, a red toboggan – his hands in his pockets, a faraway expression on his face when picturing it. He had spotted the toboggan in the window of a second-hand shop, when wandering down a cobblestone lane leading off from the square. From that moment on, he harboured a craving, particularly in the present wintry conditions. He wanted it so much and could think of nothing else, especially so near when in the square.

'You're very quiet, James. Is anything the matter?' Malcolm asked, his curiosity aroused.

'Nothin' really, it's just …' James in a melancholy mood, looking on the ground, wondering if it was still there. Suppose someone had bought it. 'Tis just that, I wos thinking of a toboggin', a red one,' he added for good measure.

'A present for Christmas?' said Malcolm, a twinkle in his eye.

His eyes as big as saucers, James looking up met Malcolm's gaze, ''Ow did 'e know, I ain't told no one?' Confused and embarrassed, he looked away. ''E couldn't, 'e's just teasin' ain't 'e?'

For a while, they walked around the relatively empty square in a silence broken by James, who exclaimed, 'Looks, it's stopped snowin'.'

Sure enough, as quickly as it had started, it had now stopped, a Christmas-card scene frozen in time, brightly lit shop fronts in the gathering dusk, crammed with last minute purchases, with notices giving forthcoming sales. Shafts of light paved their way across churned-up snow muddied by so many feet. The Christmas tree, its boughs weighed down, its coloured lights vibrant, in a league of its own.

Nearing the edge of the square, Malcolm paused. Laying his hand on James' shoulder, he smiled. 'I've been thinking,' he said, 'anyone who wants a toboggan at a time like this should have one, don't you think?'

Not knowing what to make of the remark, James didn't reply.

'I must leave you now, I've things to do.' Malcolm, seeing a puzzled expression on James' face, commented, 'Don't you worry, I'm sure everything will be alright. Merry Christmas James, and you too Dog.' He bent and ruffled the dog's ears. Turning on his heels, before disappearing down a side street, he waved.

By himself, James, now finding the square not so attractive, was beginning to see it for what it was – devoid of people, cold, bleak and inhospitable. Even the Christmas tree was looking sorry for itself.

'Well Dog, I ain't sure what 'e wos goin' on 'bout, but I ain't goin' to worry 'bout it.'

The dog wagging his tail when hearing his name, his amber eyes as always fixed on James' face.

'Come on, let's go 'ome,' he gasped, laughing, with Dog, ever willing to please, jumping up to thrust a whiskery nose in his face.

Chapter 31

A serene night, a starlit night, with no evidence of the moon, but dominated by a single star, had drawn to a close. With the dawn, inhabitants of the sleepy market town of Stonebridge awaking from their slumbers. In treetops and shrubberies, hungry birds up and about competed in their quest for worms.

The market square, half in shadow, catching the morning sun, was now silent in its lonely vigil. In its centre stood the Christmas tree, slowly shedding an icy burden, melting and running in rivulets over cobblestones into drains. Rooftops blanketed in snow, with the rays of a weak sun shining on windowpanes, where icicles had formed, water dripped down gullies.

On the outskirts, a sound of church bells, their peals echoed over frost-encrusted meadowland and fields; sheep in a huddle fed off winter hay. The town was coming to life, with groups of people all making their way in the same direction, intent on sharing a first Christmas service.

Slowly up the garden path, Tibby padding on velvet paws, an old cat now and not so sure. Ignored by all and sundry in the frantic preparations leading up to Christmas, she had spent the night in the henhouse, much to the discomfort of its inhabitants, only leaving, tail erect, her warm bed of straw, when rudely awakened at daybreak by the persistent crowing of the cockerel.

She was now on her way up the path, mewing as hearing the sound of church bells, with the declared aim of a bite to eat and the warm confines of her basket.

Mary too, aroused from her slumbers on hearing the church bells, was thinking of food and the day ahead. Sitting up in bed and rubbing the sleep out of her eyes, she glanced at the bedside clock, finding, to her horror, it was later than she thought. Beside her, Charles still in the land of nod. Downstairs the sound of a movement and a clatter of crockery urged her to slip out of bed and draw back the curtains. Up and about, having dressed, she cried, 'Charles wake up!' With no response, prodding him in the ribs, Charles opened his eyes, for a moment trying to get his bearings.

''Tis early, wot be goin' on about now, woman?'

''Tis Christmas day an' time to git up, fer heaven's sake, stir yer stumps. Amelia needs 'elp in the kitchen, 'er can't do all the work.' Opening the window, and letting in the crisp morning air, she shivered. Blinded by the sun, she turned away.

'But ain't it all prepared? I peeled the spuds meself. Wot a fuss 'bout nothing. You go on, I'll join 'e in a minute.'

'Promise 'e won't go back to bed.'

'Come to think on it, I wos having a lovely dream,' said Charles, a twinkle in his eye.

'Oh, go on with 'e!' Mary exclaimed as leaving the room.

In the kitchen Amelia, standing by the range, looked up as Mary appeared.

'Us overslept; 'tis an old alarm, an' it didn't go off,' she told her by way of an explanation. 'It ain't no excuse fer not bein' up and about.' Mary frowned. 'I wos 'oping to go to church.'

'You run along, I can cope, but 'e won't 'ave any time fer breakfast but fer a fresh pot of tea on the hob.'

'But I can't leave 'e wi ...'

'Go!' Amelia pointed to the door.

*

In the church porch, to the clamour of church bells, Jeremiah Makepiece, bending down to take of his bicycle clips, on hearing a discreet cough, looked up to find standing in the doorway a young woman. A stranger by all accounts – someone in need of help, by the worried expression on her face. 'Can I help you, my dear?' with a friendly smile he asked, getting to his feet.

Returning his smile, she replied, 'Yes please, my name's Tammy. I don't usually go to Church, but as it's Christmas I ...'

'My dear, everyone is welcomed in God's house, especially

at this time of year.'

'I'm not late, am I?' she asked, the smile fading from her lips.

'No, please take a seat inside,' the vicar indicated an inner door, slightly ajar. 'You'll find a number of the congregation in there already. I shall be going in in a moment myself.' His eyes widening on hearing a crunch of shoes on the gravel path, swinging around, he exclaimed, 'Wait! Here's someone who may keep you company.'

Singularly, their presence hadn't gone amiss. Mary, on approaching the porch and having seen the two, had recognised the young woman. It was the kennel maid, but her name had escaped her. Was it Tania or Tammy? She struggled to remember. A bright thought occurred and with it a memory, when recalling the song "Tammy's in Love".

Jeremiah, on her approach, his face creased in a benevolent smile, held out his hand. 'It's nice to see you again, I do hope you are well and the family.' On raising an enquiring eyebrow, he asked, 'By the way, how's Marjorie? Better I hope. I was so pleased to hear the news.' Not waiting for an answer, turning to Tammy, he went on to say, 'This is Tammy, who doesn't usually attend, but wishes to join us today. Would you like to keep her company?'

''Er's welcome to sit alongside of me. 'Specially 'cos us knows each other.'

*

Inside the church, rays of sunshine filtering through the stained-glass windows into a cool, dim interior, sent colours of the rainbow – oranges, reds and blues, to name but a few – colours shedding light on familiar outlines and well known faces, some kneeling in prayer. Mary and Tammy picked their way past ornamental pews, making their way up the aisle, as passing, observed by others, some nodding in acknowledgement. Mary caught sight of Oliver and Pam in a front pew, glad to have seen them, for she intended to invite them along with others to a

Christmas spread and get-together at the cottage.

With such a good turnout, having been lucky enough to find a seat, the two of them settled down. Tammy, stealing a glimpse of her surroundings, had been surprised to see people she knew, people she would have thought would not have attended, for it had been some time since she had last graced the church's interior. With memories of a childhood spent with her brother within its walls, finding it relatively unchanged, she took in the sight of a nativity scene placed not far from the altar steps, by a Christmas tree in a corner, festooned with baubles, strewn with tinsel and crowned with a golden star. Holly berries and sprigs of mistletoe encircled stone pillars. With her brother's death – he'd crashed when driving his motorcycle at speed – she nursed a grievance. She prayed for his recovery, although advised otherwise, had fumed and blamed God. Along with her parents, her heart hardened, she'd stayed away, up until now.

But listening to the sermon, now not so fixed in her opinions, not feeling so alone. With thoughts of Marjorie – how her family had rallied around in her hour of need. Of Harry, Pam's youngest son – he too, like her had been at odds with the world. They too had been tested in times of trouble. Christmas and its story of the birth of Jesus brought people together to share hopes for a brighter and better future. Perhaps Mary was thinking the same things: she had been absorbed in the sermon, and like her had enjoyed singing the carols.

Outside after the service, in a cold and frosty churchyard, Mary and Tammy were to find themselves rubbing shoulders with groups of people, talking amongst themselves, some laughing and joking with thoughts of Christmas. Wrapped up warmly against the icy conditions, others, when taking their leave, bid the vicar farewell and thanked him for the service, whilst others lingered. Mary, having caught sight of Oliver and Pam about to leave, broke away from a group near to the church porch, with Tammy quickening her step in an attempt to catch them up.

Puffing and panting, calling 'Pam! … Pam!' hoping to attract her attention, as with Oliver bidding farewell to friends and acquaintances by the lych gate

At the sound of her name, Pam's face on catching sight of Mary broadening into a smile as swinging around. 'Well I never!' she gasped, 'Fancy seeing you, we didn't see you in church. Did you enjoy the service?'

Mary, conscious of Tammy looking slightly embarrassed hovering in the background, bade her to join them.

'How's Marjorie?' Pam slightly amused at Mary's exertions, on seeing Tammy making her way over, asked, 'Who's your friend?'

''Er ain't a friend, 'er's more an acquaintance, 'er …' a sentence left in mid air, on Tammy's approach.

'I'm sorry I left 'e like that, 'e must 'ave wondered wot I be up to. … This be 'Arry Jenkins' Ma.' A puzzled expression forming on Tammy's face prompting Mary to add, 'Surely 'e remembers Marj's motorcycle accident wi' the dog. Us thinks it the same dog that chased Harry on 'e's push bike out onto the road, in front of the doctor – folks say, 'e never got over it.'

'I heard about the accident, everyone was talking about it. I'm so sorry, it must have been awful for you at the time.' Tammy hadn't known Harry to speak to, but seeing the pained look in Pam's eyes at the mention of his name, had felt a wave of emotion.

'It's all in the past now,' true to form, never one to dwell on things, said Pam, brightening up. 'One's got to move on, hasn't one? … By the way, this is my other son, Oliver, Harry's older brother, he's doing well in the family business – he took over when his father, his father …' Solemn-eyed, she pursed her lips.

'Yes I heard about that too. You've had more than your share of bad luck,' Tammy said, glancing at Oliver.

'But who's this; you haven't said?' Pam asked, giving Mary a disapproving look. 'Introduce us properly.'

Unperturbed, Mary said, 'This 'ere is Tammy, 'er's a kennel maid at the pound. 'Er came to our rescue at the hospital when us wos visitin' Marj.'

'How?' A puzzled frown creased Pam's face.

'It be a long story but I shan't tell 'e all.

On hearing this, an ever restless Oliver intervening said, 'Ma, I really must be going, you stay if you want to.'

Pushing open and passing through the gate, the three of them stood and watched his tall figure making itself purposely down the lane until disappearing out of sight. A silence prevailed, broken by Pam, who shaking her head commented, 'Another girlfriend, I hope it works out this time. I'm fed up with him sowing his wild oats.'

Mary, nodding in agreement, glancing at her wristwatch, gasped, 'Amelia, 'er'll be wondering where I am, an' the bus is gone. I'll 'ave to walk.'

'What a pity,' Pam, genuinely sorry, felt compelled to say. 'I would have given you a lift, but Oliver and I decided to walk to church for a change; I don't like driving in icy conditions, anyway. Perhaps I could walk some of the way with you and Tammy. Would you like that?'

For a while, with little to say, they picked their way down the lane, now soggy and wet with the sun's warmth, on either side, as thawing, water dripping from the hedgerows.

Jeremiah Makepiece, at that moment cycling past on his newly acquired bicycle, called out, 'Mind the puddles; I'll try not to splash you. Do have a nice Christmas.'

Breaking the silence, Tammy exclaimed, 'What a mess, I should have brought my wellies.'

As watching the vicar cycling down the lane, Pam, turning to Mary, asked, 'Now what were you talking about earlier on? You didn't finish what you were saying, something about Tammy rescuing you, wasn't it?'

Not wanting to be the centre of attention, breaking in, Tammy protested: 'It wasn't anything like that. I didn't do anything. I was simply there at the time.'

'Yes,' said Mary, 'but 'e wos concerned.'

'I still don't know what you're talking about, let me in on it, do!' Pam, overwhelmed with curiosity, exclaimed, for the conversation seemed to be leading nowhere.

Together they walked on, Mary telling Pam how she, Charlie and Amelia on a visit to the hospital had found James apparently alone in the ward with Marjorie. With pandemonium in the hospital corridors and a dog on the run, how Tammy, a nurse and a male orderly trying to catch it, on finding their way to the ward, having seen it emerging from under the bed, had tried to grab it without success. She told of its mounting fear when picking up on James' change of mood and body language, with the clatter of an overturned chair, knocked over by the orderly standing in front of the door, impeding any means of escape. Their desperate attempts to restrain a dog rushing wildly around the room, barking frantically; of the noise, the sound of which, it seemed, had brought about a miracle, one they'd prayed for – the awakening of Marjorie from a comatose sleep.

''E wos visiting a sick friend,' Mary said, ''ow is 'er?'

'Still quite ill, but there has been a slight improvement,' Tammy responded, soulfully.

'Amelia seemed to think 'e knew the dog's history.'

'Yes I did, but I was …'

'Visitin' yer friend who's poorly. Can 'e tell us 'bout it now?'

'Why, yes of course.' Tammy, stopping to break a twig from the hedgerow, paused. Studying it, she reflected, her eyes taking on a faraway look, that of another place, another time, her face brightening up as visualizing a moment peculiar to her. 'Yes,' she cried, 'I remember the day they brought them in, as if it were only yesterday. We couldn't tell them apart, they were so alike, but we were soon to learn they were very different in temperament, although from the same litter.' She paused.

'Yes, do go on,' prompted Pam. 'I was just getting interested, and then what happened?'

'Due to the breakdown of his marriage, and intending to work abroad, their owner, heartbroken, left the pound in tears, not once looking back. Initially, both dogs pined for their master, refusing to eat, but with the passage of time, giving up any hope of his return, came into their own. That is when they revealed their true personalities. Charlie grieved for his owner and had a tendency to howl at night, but Rover handled the loss of their master in a different way. One day a kennel maid not securing the catch on the wire door, he made good his escape, hiding by the main gates until the time was ripe. An escape not discovered until feeding and mucking-out time. Charlie left to his devices, although distressed, making no attempt to follow in his errant brother's paw prints.

In the ensuring days, with a hue and cry with sightings of Rover, some imaginary, others real, the latter of a dog spotted alternatively scratching and barking at the door of a house with a "For Sale" sign in its overgrown garden. Talk amongst villagers of the dog evading capture, of a dog warden losing heart, coming home empty-handed after scouring streets, alleyways, fields and surrounding countryside, spread like wildfire. Rover, streetwise, always some way ahead, becoming aggressive and unapproachable. In the pound, their temporary home, Charlie grieving for his long-lost brother, refusing to eat ... Then ...

'What happened?' Pam's eyes danced with excitement.

'All alone, Charlie, dear Charlie grieved. He pushed his dish away at feeding time and barely drunk any water. But lay, nose on paws, ears twitching, brown eyes fixed on the wrought iron gates, his consequent loss of weight and zest for life giving cause for concern. That is until ...'

'That is until what?' cried Pam, all ears by her side, Mary agog.

'That is until ...' Tammy, herself emotionally affected by the memory of a handsome dog, now dead, with the demise of Harry Jenkins, drew in her breath. Saddened by the thought, pulling herself together, she went on to say, 'Until Ruby ...'

'Ruby, James' sister, what's she got to do with it?'

'Charlie took to her right away and started eating again, much to our relief. Neither she nor I know why, perhaps it some sound, smell or tone of voice that triggered it off, we'll never know.'

In the distance, the church clock struck the hour. A worried frown creased Mary's brow, as glancing at her watch. 'It ain't,' she took another look. ''Tis, I best be going; Amelia worries. 'Er

155

will think something's 'appened to me, but the story and them dogs, me heart bleeds fer 'em.'

'I'm sorry, I shouldn't have kept you, but you wanted to know the dog's history. Perhaps I went on too long,' said Tammy, her cheeks a rosy pink.

'No it ain't yer fault, 'tis mine. I wanted to 'ear, and now I 'ave. But I'd best be goin' home now.'

'Yes, so must I.' Pam, indicating a branch in the road, asked Tammy, 'Are you going in my direction?'

Grateful for her company, Tammy replied, 'That would be nice.'

'Perhaps 'e'd both like to join us fer a get together at the cottage, 'bout four this afternoon?' Mary said before going her separate way.

Could the dog be the one who had caused the motorcycle accident, the one who had chased Harry out onto the road on that fateful day, could it be one of the same? ... Could it have been Rover? Was Pam thinking the same thing? She hadn't said anything – Mary wondered why, these thoughts uppermost in her mind, as hurrying along home.

Chapter 32

The late morning sun lay peacefully on the kitchen table scrubbed diligently by Amelia, its rays kissing the best silver cutlery laid out in readiness on the newly laundered tablecloth for the Christmas Day lunch. In a corner Tibby was curled up, her pink nose twitching, her gastric juices stimulated, delectable smells wafting from the oven. The kettle whistled, steam filling the kitchen, dissipating with Amelia coming in from the garden, letting in a rush of cold air.

Washing her hands at the sink, tired, she sat down on a kitchen chair, trying to collect her thoughts. Relieved that everything as far as she knew was ready, and quite proud of her efforts, her thoughts switched to Mary. Where was she? She had asked Charles, whom she had left reading, sitting by the window in the parlour, to keep an eye out for her, and let her know should she appear. She might as well make some tea for herself and Charles, there was no point in worrying, Mary would be bound to turn up sooner or later. She consoled herself with the thought. Gently prising open the parlour door, which she had found ajar, with her foot, she saw that Charles had fallen asleep, his spectacles having slipped down over his nose, the book he had been reading lying open on the floor. On a nearby table, she placed the tray of tea and biscuits and, bending down, picking up the book, replaced the marker. 'Charles, can you hear me?' she asked, touching him on the shoulder, but he only grunted. So she left the room, closing the door quietly behind her.

Outside in the passageway, as passing the hall mirror, momentarily aware of her reflection, instinctively drawn, she stopped to scrutinize her image. Iron-grey hair drawn back from a careworn face, blue-grey eyes, solemn and pensive, meeting her gaze from under a lined brow. Looking down at work-hardened hands, freckled with age spots, at the thin golden wedding band, now embedded, an accepted part of her, she visualised times when these same hands were slender and unmarked, her long auburn hair unchecked, cascading down her shoulders, her face unlined and figure trim. Memories came flooding back of unbearable grief with her husband's sudden death some years ago. A tear trickled down her cheek. She missed Edward, but life goes on. Not one to dwell on the past, Amelia mentally chastised herself for such indulgent thoughts that generally materialised at Christmas. All the more reason to enjoy the Festive Season, perhaps memories like these best left in the past, she thought, as switching on the coloured lights so carefully arranged by Mary around the mirror, now with a kaleidoscope of colours circling the darkened hall, as if in a frenzied dance.

All was well in the kitchen, so picking up a newspaper, with the intention of joining Charles, she was just slipping out of her flowery wrap-over and patting her hair in place when the phone in the hall rang.

On lifting the receiver, 'Who's speakin'?' she asked, with a feeling of foreboding when hearing a woman's voice.

'I'm speaking from the hospital, my name is Dr Soper. Can I speak to Mrs Mary Henderson, please?'

Amelia suddenly felt cold, a feeling of inadequacy engulfed her, as if paralysed on the spot, the unexpected call filling her with dread as fearing the worst.

'It ain't, it ain't Marj … is it?' Her voice, ineffective and tremulous, to her didn't measure up.

'I'm afraid the matter can't be discussed over the phone and even then only with the next of kin, or better still at the hospital.' With a certain amount of sympathy, the Doctor stuck to her guns. And with that, with a click at the end of the phone and the line going dead, the caller had gone.

'Wos that the phone?' Charles in his wheelchair, nudging the parlour door open in an effort to guide it through, seeing her so distraught, stopped and applied the brake. 'Wot's wrong, 'as something 'appened to our Mary?'

The sight of him filled Amelia with remorse. Seeing him

sat there in his chair, so vulnerable and yet so compassionate, tears falling freely down her cheeks, she knelt down beside him, laying her head on his shoulder, there to find solace in his thick woolly cardigan. Her breath coming out in gasps, trying to communicate, her voice was muted, Charles with a protective arm around her, at times not knowing what she was trying to say.

'It's, I think …'

'Our Mary?' Charles' eyes widened. ''As 'er bin in an accident?'

She raised her head, her eyes met his. Charles, taking out a handkerchief, wiped her tear-stained face. Choking back the sobs, she cried, 'No Charles, it ain't Mary, 'tis Marj.'

'Marj? Wot's happened to 'er?'

Amelia, getting up, straightened her skirt. Pulling down her cardigan, she said, ''Er didna say. The doc wouldna tell me anything. 'Er could 'ave spoken to you. I didna think to ask.'

'Wot's 'er name?'

'Doctor Soper, 'er wanted to speak to our Mary.'

'On Christmas Day! Anyway, our Marj is in a safe place, us must wait 'til Mary shows up. 'Til then, 'ow 'bout a nice cup of tea?'

'But I brought 'e in some.'

'I ain't drinking stone-cold tea. Come on, smile,' Charles coaxed. Seeing her doleful expression, he exclaimed, 'When 'e do, yer face lights up!'

Chapter 33

'That was some turkey, Ma, I really enjoyed it; the Brussels sprouts weren't cooked, there again, Dad likes them that way, sort of crisp, so we all suffer.' Ruby seeing the guarded look on her mother's face, smiled. 'I couldn't have eaten another mouthful.'

'Yes, it was quite a meal, still it's only once a year. I got the turkey from the farmer, you know, the one we buy our eggs off. Did you notice how James wolfed his down; he'll get indigestion if he doesn't look out. Talking of James, where is he, Rube? We don't want to be late for Mary's party. Get him to wash and comb his hair when you find. Tell him to smarten himself up, wear a tie. I don't want him turning up in a pair of dirty old jeans, sweat shirt and down-at-heel plimsolls, like last time.' Marian beamed, her daughter never held grudges, although observing her offspring together, James may well have thought otherwise.

'I don't know where he gets to,' Ruby sighed. 'Last time I saw him, he was going to the lav.' Ruby, stepping to the kitchen window, looked out onto the back garden at a granite outhouse at the top of the path. 'The door's shut – he's probably in there now, dead to the world, reading a comic.'

'Wherever, he is, tell him to get a move on. I've got Dad's shirt to iron, amongst other things. Anything for you?'

'Thanks Ma, there's no need, it's all done and dusted.'

*

James, rummaging in the front parlour, looked up as Ruby came in.

'Lost something?' she asked, biting her tongue when seeing the untidy mess he'd created.

'Dog's lead.'

'When you've found it, I hope you'll put all those things back, before you have your wash and brush up. Ma wants you to wear your best suit for Aunt Mary's party. Dad's outside, chaining the car wheels, just to be on the safe side – there may still be icy patches. Where's Dog anyway?'

''Ow should I know?' A gloomy James, piling up a number of items scattered around the carpet into an untidy heap, offloaded them into a cupboard.

'You should, it's your dog.' Ruby felt her hackles rise. 'You'd better find Dog, and double quick, else there'll be ructions.'

'It ain't my fault. Dog won' keep still, it ain't like 'im.'

'What do you expect me to do, you wanted him? Go and find him and hurry up about it.'

'Wot fer? I don' want to go to a silly ole party, them's far too old. Them's boring. Dad wouldna go but fer the beer.'

'So I'm old, am I and boring? Well, thank you very much. You've got to come, it's expected, do you hear me? Go on you cheeky monkey, before I box your ears, and find that dog!'

Hands in his pockets, a sullen expression on his face, James slouched off, muttering under his breath, 'I'm not goin'.'

Ruby, watching him from the parlour window, turned her head when hearing her mother's voice. 'What did you say, Ma?'

'Is that our James?'

'Yes, Ma.'

'What's wrong now?'

'He says he's lost Dog.'

'He better find him, I hope he's dressed up for the weather.'

James, feeling sorry for himself, pensive, scuffed up the snow with his boots, as traipsing along. Stopping to take his bearing, he had a brainwave – they, particularly Ruby, didn't think he'd be going to the party, but he'd surprise them by being there when they arrived. By then, not coming home, they'd be frantic with worry, but finding him they'd be relieved, and he'd be the centre of attention. Smugly, he inwardly congratulated himself, muttering, 'I ain't jist a pretty face.' Then brightening up, his thoughts turned to Dog, the cause of his demise, 'You wait till I finds 'e; 'e'll know who's boss.'

*

A solitary figure sat on wet hospital steps leading down to a sodden car park, now relatively empty. A wide expanse of forecourt forsaken by the sun, a cold, dismal aspect under a grey forbidding sky. A place over which lighted windows cast elongated shafts of light.

A cold wind ruffled the dog's fur, as restless, he changed position, panting loudly, his breath clouding the freezing air, then feeling the chill, whining, choosing to lie down. There he lay, nose on paws, tail tucked between legs, amber eyes registering disapproval, ears twitching on hearing the slamming of doors, sirens and the sound of voices.

Sitting in the taxi, her heart pounding, Mary, rubbing the condensation off the window with a gloved hand, peered out. A speeding panorama of woods and fields met her eyes, a winter wonderland, with snow thawing, residues of water running off fields on either side, flooding the narrower lanes. Dotted here and there, silhouettes of cottages, farms and outbuildings, with Christmas lights sparkling in the gathering dusk. In no time at all, with the hospital coming into view, the taxi having rounded a corner and driven through the gates, Mary, with mixed emotions, clenched her hands, her knuckles white with the effort.

Momentarily, in the subdued light, the taxi's headlights picked out a stone pillar, behind which on hearing and seeing it approach, Malcolm had hidden, taking refuge in its shadow.

As the taxi passed, peering out from his vantage point, he saw through the passenger window a face, a familiar face – it was Mary's, she was looking distraught and ill at ease. With a solemn expression, he watched as the taxi pulled up and stopped in front of the hospital steps, before slipping out through the gates and onto the road.

Preoccupied, Mary, unaware of Dog's presence when alighting from the taxi and mounting the steps, didn't react, as Dog, standing on all fours, snuffled in recognition, his tail wagging appreciatively.

Picking up, having read her body language, he watched her enter. Alone again, resuming his former position, oblivious to the occasional pat, he remained at his post, now and then, as if disturbed by some sixth sense, whimpering and pawing the air.

Eventually, on recognising her scent and the sound of her voice, as the swing doors opened, rising from his haunches, shaking himself vigorously, Dog watched and waited. Although making his presence known and again ignored, on interpreting her mood and finding it a happier one, as if in harmony, ears pricked, tail wagging, he barked enthusiastically.

Attracted by the noise, Mary, looking back as the taxi drove away, caught a glimpse of Dog standing on the steps. Dog, as the vehicle's tail lights disappeared from sight, intent on following, padded down the steps.

Chapter 34

Laying back in her chair, Mary closed her eyes, relishing the quiet atmosphere, a serenity broken only by the tic toc of the kitchen clock. 'It's bin a long day, an' a tirin' one, but worth it, don' 'e think?' she said, soothed by its steady momentum.

'I never felt so 'appy.' Charles, sat opposite beside the kitchen range, knocked out his pipe on the fender. 'I told 'e there wos nothing to worry 'bout, barring …' He paused, avoiding her gaze.

'Barring … wot do 'e mean by that?' A haunted look in her eye, she studied his face.

'Nothin' I wos jist thinkin'.' Charles, wishing to evade the subject he unwittingly had raised, tried to dismiss it out of hand. Manoeuvring his chair closer to the range, he prised open the cast-iron door to poke the dying embers.

'Wot?' Mary frowned.

'If 'e must know, that it's 'bout time I went up the wooden hill by meself without yer 'elp, but that will never 'appen will it?'

Mary, never one to fudge the truth, a fixed look on her face, for a while sat staring into the fire. The light fading, flames coming to life, flickering, shadowy images dancing on the rough-cast walls, her mind drifted back to happier times. In the corner, the tree caught her eye. Garlanded with tinsel, baubles dangling from branches, rich with a smell of pine, coloured lights enhanced and twinkling in the dim light, the very essence of Christmas prompting her to say, 'Us got each other, us is luckier than some. Ain't that true? An' our Marj. 'Er is on the up and up. Jist think 'ow Pam feels without 'er 'Arry this Christmas.'

'Wot would I do without 'e, yer me guardian angel.' Charles gave a loving look.

'Oh, go on wi' 'e.' Mary blushed.

'Ow 'bout a glass of wine fer me guardian angel?' he cajoled, and smugly, 'An' 'ow 'bout another beer fer me?'

Watching Charles pour out the wine, Mary said, 'Us 'ave come this far. It ain't good, but it could be worse. Tis brought us together; together us must ride the storm. Us got friends and family, ain't us, more than some. Count yer blessings. Anyways, I'm not dwellin' on the past; I'm lookin' to the future. It wos good to see Tim, 'e could 'ave let us know 'e'd be comin . T'was a pity I wos out. Still 'e didna come 'ome to an empty cottage, with Amelia 'ere and 'e 'olding the fort. Soon 'e will be 'ome again fer good, that's somethin' to look forward to, ain't it Charles? Charles, I've bin talkin' 'bout Tim, yer not listenin', I've bin talkin' to meself!'

Charles, who'd been napping, opened his eyes, grunted and closed them again, still clutching the empty beer bottle in his hand. Mary gentle prised it away and placed it on the table.

Standing there, regarding the lined brow, the grey hair thinning at the temples, the same old pullover he always wore "because it was comfortable", the blanket thrown carelessly over his knees, under which peeped carpet slippers – a present from her some Christmases ago – she felt a wave of compassion. 'Wot ever am I goin' to do with 'e Charles? Dear Charles, 'e's so easily hurt an' yet so proud.'

A lingering smell of cigars pervaded the air as Mary bent down in an attempt to tidy up perceived fragments of a discarded cracker lying under the table. Crouching to pick them up triggered memories – memories of voices and movement in the kitchen, now empty, but only a few hours ago full of familiar faces. Tim and Ruby had waged a mock tug of war on this very spot. Amused, she had stood and watched them, trying to read some meaning into their facial expressions but failing to do so. Under the Christmas tree, James, to his delight, had found a large parcel addressed to him. Discovered by Amelia on the doorstep sometime that afternoon, mystified, she had brought it in and placed it there. On opening it, and very excited on discovering a red toboggan – just what he'd wanted – James had cried, 'Well it ain't from Father Christmas, 'cos there ain't one, I knows that now, but it could be …' Left alone with his prize and unquestioned, he hadn't finished the sentence.

'It's a veritable feast!' Pam had exclaimed at the sight of a kitchen table fully laden with Christmas fare. Plates of sandwiches of all descriptions, savoury flans, cocktail sausages on sticks, sausage rolls, jelly and ice-cream, trifle and custard, Christmas cake – 'Yes, a gourmet's delight,' she had said, casting her eyes over the tempting display. She eyed James with some amusement, catching him at random stuffing some of the goodies in his trouser pockets "for a rainy day", on the pretext of keeping them back for Dog.

Dog, however, seemed to be doing very well. James and Tammy, after an exhaustive search, had found him not far from the cottage, somewhat dejected, supposedly making his way home. Now thoroughly spoiled by all and sundry, he'd been padding from lap to lap, from person to person, Tibby watching with rounded eyes from the safety of Amelia's lap, with Dog, unaware of her presence, padding by. Restless, kneading her paws, she had jumped down, seeking refuge behind Charles' wheelchair. Eventually enticing her out with a morsel from his plate, he had remarked, 'Fer a long while, 'er wouldna come near me. Now look, 'er's takin' titbits off me.'

Meanwhile, Pam, a picture of sophistication, her blonde hair piled high, sitting legs crossed, had been in earnest conversation with Tim for a while. Attired in the latest line from the boutique, her slender fingers clasping a long cigarette holder from which smoke spiralled, she'd only had eyes for him.

Ruby, with mixed feelings, watching them from a distance, like Oliver, had been glad when hearing her say, 'It's time to go, does anyone want a lift?' Oliver, out of place and bored, had been twiddling his fingers most of the time. Ruby, who had been looking forward to meeting up with Tim, had hardly got to know him, with Pam monopolising the time.

'Yes please,' Tammy had said, for she had the dogs to exercise, their kennels to clean – all of them were to be bedded down with clean straw for the night. Life went on just the same at the pound.

'We'd better go too; 'early to bed, early to rise, makes a man healthy, wealthy and wise,' so I've been led to believe, … women too, I hope.' Ruby's mother winked at all and sundry. 'And you as well.' She beckoned a truculent daughter who, given the chance, would have liked to linger, but hadn't wanted to get involved in an argument, especially in front of Tim. To an inebriated husband smiling foolishly, she commented, 'I might have known, I suppose I better take the wheel.'

'Thanks for the lift.' Tammy hadn't relished walking home in the dark by herself.

'You're welcome, there's plenty of room.' Pam glancing at Tim, on catching his eye, mouthed "goodbye". So he was on leave, she'd thought, but for how long?

Mary, having helped them on with their coats and scarves and waved them goodbye, had been standing on the front doorstep when the telephone rang. Quaking inwardly, thinking, *No not more bad news,* she'd lifted the receiver. It was the hospital, but not the bad news she had expected – it was the best. Marjorie, discharged, would be coming home in the New Year for good. Arrangements had been made for her aftercare and there was simply nothing more to worry about. Or was there?

Where was Malcolm? At the party that afternoon, she had had a golden opportunity to ask Oliver, but hadn't taken it.

*

With the cottage coming into sight, Malcolm had been somewhat relieved to see no one around. On finding the garden gate resistant, he had placed the parcel on the adjoining wall, in an attempt to free it. Swollen, it refused to budge, but finally, complaining loudly, had relented, breaking the silence. Not wanting to be seen at this stage, Malcolm, having glanced furtively around, was relieved when still finding no one about. No one at the window, no one outside in the garden, not even Tibby. Reassured, he had made his way up the path to the front door. Placing the parcel on the step, he had quietly retraced his steps, taking care to close the gate with a minimum of noise. Most probably, he would call in on his way back from the hospital. With this thought in mind, he had set off. With the hospital coming into sight, he found, when passing through the wrought iron gates, a comparatively empty car park and forecourt.

A dog had been sitting on the steps, near to the main entrance. Undeterred by his sudden appearance, seemingly unaware, it had risen on its haunches, its eyes focused on the road outside. Fascinated by its vigilance, and drawn by its strange behaviour, Malcolm, suddenly struck by its appearance, its similarity to James' dog, had wondered what it was doing there. Not knowing what to think, nor what to do, he'd lost interest. He hadn't wanted to make a fool of himself; to him most dogs looked alike, anyway.

With thoughts of Marjorie – how he would find her, and what he would say after such a long time? – he had bought some flowers from a kiosk. Was this the right time to tell her how he really felt? Was any time the right time? His life on hold, a solitary one with no meaning, was the accident his fault? If so, a price he would have to pay, or should he just turn his back, forget all about it and walk away? One way or another, he must make up his mind. Mustering up courage, about to enter, distracted by the sound of an engine, he had looked over his shoulder to see a taxi approaching at speed. Out of curiosity, he dodged behind a pillar to see who it was, his heart missing a beat when seeing a familiar face.

Mary, in the back seat, had looked preoccupied and ill at ease. Had Marjorie taken a turn for the worse? He watched her alight – indifferent to the dog's entreaties, she had passed it by. Alone again, the dog subdued, resuming his former position, had laid down, eyes closed, ears pricked, outwardly alert.

Malcolm, his mind in a quandary, turned his back. *What now?* he had thought, as walking away. All the plans of mice and men and all that – now, fate had taken a hand, and not kindly, curtailing his visit to wipe the slate clean. Thwarted, he had found himself in a dilemma.

Later, on hearing voices when near to the cottage, seeing Pam's car parked outside behind another car, he had endeavoured to appear inconspicuous.

Concealed in the shrubberies fringing the road, he had watched Mary on the front step waving goodbye, with Pam's car and its occupants rounding the bend. From his vantage point, he had watched Ruby, by the garden gate in the throes of a heated argument with her mother, her face a picture of misery, climb into the car.

No one seemed happy, even though it was Christmas Day. With this sobering thought, having watched the car drive off, he had set off down the lane.

*

The train shunting out of the station and gathering momentum, Malcolm, sat by the carriage window, his heart on his sleeve, watched for the last time the flickering lights of the little market town, merging with the darkening landscape, disappear, leaving him with only his own image reflected in the darkened window.

He reached up, pulling down his briefcase from the overhanging rack. He sat down, and taking out a note pad and pen, he started to write.

Chapter 35

At the stroke of midnight, the clamour of church bells broke the silence. Numerous fireworks whizzed skywards, peaking and effecting spectacular explosions, cascading in multi-coloured sparks.

This prompted Dog to nudge open the door and scamper out onto the path. Panic stricken, Ruby followed, and as he stopped by the gate, put on his lead. To her surprise, he didn't attempt to resist, but docile, just stood there as if to say, "What's the panic about?"

'You're a funny dog,' said Ruby, as Dog, encouraged, nudged her persuasively, pleading for a caress, 'but the best friend James has ever had.'

For a short while, it seemed as if all the inhabitants of Stonebridge had gathered together for a meeting of minds. In the alleyways, cul-de-sacs and roadways, everywhere they came out in strength to welcome in the New Year. The square in its centre, the lighted Christmas tree now shedding its needles, around which individuals walked and talked in groups as excited children ran around or simply stood, faces upturned, watching the display, some clutching and waving sparklers.

But all things come to an end. Little by little, the crowds thinning out as, homeward bound, leaving behind a silence broken only by drunken revellers spilling out onto the road from various public houses.

'Do 'e want to go back in the warm, Charles? 'Tis the last of the fireworks. T'was worth seein', don't 'e think? Pity our Marj didna see it; still, 'er's 'ome now, 'er best take one day at a time.'

''Tis 'bout time, I suppose, to call it a day,' Charles said, in an endeavour to manoeuvre his wheelchair over a cracked flagstone towards the kitchen door.

'Shall I give 'e a push?' Mary, on seeing Charles' reaction, not to be deterred, added, 'I know 'e likes to do it by yerself, but a little 'elp, at times goes a long way.'

'Where's Amelia?' asked Charles, looking around. 'I 'aven't seen 'er fer ages.'

''Er's in bed, where us should be, 'er went up ages ago.' Mary frowned. ''Ave 'e seen Tibby? I 'ope 'er wasn't scared wi' the noise.'

''Er'll be alright, 'er 'as found somewhere safe, don' 'e worry.' Charles smiled at what he considered a caring, thoughtful woman. 'Let's go in, I want 'e to 'elp me up them stairs.'

*

It had been a long and tiring day, but one tinged with hope as the New Year beckoned. Mary, wishing to be alone to reflect at such a poignant time, didn't join Charles. To her it seemed that life was like a seesaw with ups and downs – that is, from despair to hope and so on. She felt Charles, although at times despondent, had at last come to terms with his disability. Pam had found a new life and moved on. Ruby, it seemed, was attracted to Tim … and thinking of Tim, where was he? – she hadn't seen him all day. But she shouldn't complain, just be glad now he was home. And Marjorie? She would look in on her before she turned in. But what about the letter?

She took it out of her apron pocket and seeing it was crumpled, straightened it out. *When Marjorie has sufficiently recovered,* she thought, *I'll give it to her.* Her thoughts fancy free, now switching to Tim who would be bedding down on the Lilo. Would he be comfortable? Had she given him her spare key to let himself in? She reached for the old jug on the mantelpiece and was relieved to find it empty.

A quarter to one, time to go up, she thought, crossing to the window. It was a calm night, not a leaf stirred. At the bottom of the garden she could distinctly pick out the old oak tree, wrapped in a silvery glow, as beyond its network of branches a pale moon emerged. Before pulling the curtains, she stood awestruck by its beauty; then, her hand to her mouth, yawning, she climbed the stairs. Outside Marjorie's room she paused, lifted the latch and peeped in. Through the windowpanes, shafts of moonlight picked out Marjorie's form as she lay there gently breathing, her face relaxed and at peace. She was home at last, where she belonged. Charles was asleep, snoring as usual. Quickly slipping off her clothes, she joined him. Exhausted as she was, she soon fell fast asleep.

*

It was the cockerel that woke Marjorie the next morning. The sun streaming through the window, she was fully awake when hearing the clatter of crockery outside the door. The door opened a crack, with Mary saying softly, 'Marj is 'e awake, I've brought 'e some tea?'

Attempting to sit up, Marjorie replied, 'Yes Ma.'

'Let me 'elp 'e,' said Mary, placing the tray on the bedside, then lifting her up in the bed.

'Is it really the New Year?' asked Marjorie, shielding her eyes from the sun. 'What a pity I missed the fireworks.'

'Never mind, 'e's 'ome fer good. Count yer blessin's. I ain't sorry to see the last of an 'orrible year,' said Mary, pulling the curtains across a little to stop the glare. 'Let's 'ope this one will be an 'appier one.'

*

A week later, Marjorie, with a little help, was taking the air at the bottom of the garden. Amelia seated beside her in companionable silence, in front of the gnarled trunk of the old oak tree reading a newspaper. After a while, glancing at Marjorie and rising rather awkwardly from her chair, she commented, 'I best see wot Mary's doin', 'er might need some 'elp. By the way, 'er asked me to give 'e this.' Before setting off up the path, taking out the crumpled letter, she handed it to Marjorie, saying at the same time, 'Mind 'e don't git cold, t'will be time fer 'e to go in soon.'

Why it's several days old, thought Marjorie, glancing at the postmark, *but the writing's familiar.* She would have recognised that spidery scrawl anywhere – it was from Malcolm. Why was he writing to her? There was only one way to find out. Her heart pounding in anticipation, her hands shaking, she slit open the envelope and drew out the contents. Leaning over the arm of the chair, she retrieved the letter, which, having fallen down, was in danger of being blown away by a light breeze. Composed, tentatively she unfolded it, reading as follows:

> Dear Marjorie,
>
> You probably must have been wondering why you haven't seen me. It hasn't been easy; I've never been able to express myself in the way that other people can. So after several attempts to put pen to paper, with misgivings, I have written the following.
>
> When you read this letter, I shall probably be far away and you may never see me again. I think this is for the best.
>
> Meeting you the way I did at the time fulfilled a need, maybe a selfish one. Because of this I shall always feel in part responsible although not at fault for the accident. I now feel it is in both our interests to part company. We've only known each other for a short time but believe me, those days were some of the happiest I have ever known. But it wasn't meant to be, over so soon, cut short by such unforeseen circumstances, it brought me back to reality.
>
> I have no doubt in time you will meet someone who will make you far happier in the long run than I ever could.
>
> Please forgive me,
>
> Malcolm.

For a while, Marjorie sat staring into space. Tears welling up, her pride hurt, angrily she screwed up the letter and threw it on the ground. Bending her head and covering her face in the palms of her hands, she wept uncontrollably. 'Why … why,' she gasped between sobs, her shoulders heaving, 'does it always happen to me?' Malcolm had written to her; she wished he hadn't. Any hopes she had of a brighter future, of picking up where they had left off, dashed.

Totally absorbed in her grief, she suddenly became aware of a movement. She watched through eyes misted with tears, Tibby, mewing, pitifully picking her way down the path. Just like her, Tibby had her grievances. The sun coming out from behind a cloud casting its warm glow, she closed her eyes.

The old cat, on reaching her, before settling down, rubbed her scrawny head against the side of the basket chair. Marjorie, feeling an empathy, muttered sleepily through half-closed lids, 'You must be hungry.'

'Yes, I could do with a bite, I'm starving.' Startled, Marjorie gripped the arm of the chair. Like the Cheshire Cat in Lewis Carroll's *Alice in Wonderland*, had Tibby the power of speech?

Of course not, the voice must be a figment of her imagination … and yet so real.

On opening her eyes, blinded by the sun, at first not discerning and then not believing what she saw, dumbstruck, she gasped. Standing in front of her, with his back to the sun, was Malcolm.

'I had no idea there was someone there … I must have dropped off.!' With mixed emotions and an element of suspicion, she cried 'Anyway, what are you doing here? From what you said in your letter, you thought we'd be better apart!'

'I should never have sent that letter. Will you ever forgive me?' He looked downtrodden and ill at ease. 'I've missed you, more that I can say.'

'How do you know I haven't met someone who would make me happier in the long run,' she retorted. Malcolm looking crestfallen, casting aside her pride and mustering up a smile, she glanced at her watch. 'Is it that time already? Time for something to eat. Tibby's told me so in no uncertain terms. We can't let good food go to waste can we? With a little bit of luck, there may even be some left over for you.'

Lightning Source UK Ltd.
Milton Keynes UK
UKOW05f1551250417
299865UK00009B/227/P